D1130368

LITTLE
BROTHER

LITTLE
BROTHER

LITTLE BROTHER

A Refugee's Odyssey

IBRAHIMA BALDE
AND AMETS ARZALLUS ANTIA

TRANSLATED FROM THE BASQUE BY
TIMBERLAKE WERTENBAKER

Arcade Publishing • New York

First North American Edition

First published in Basque as *Miñan* by Susa in 2019

This is a work of fiction. Names, places, characters, and incidents are either the
products of the author's imagination or are used fictitiously.

Arcade Publishing books may be purchased in bulk at special discounts for
sales promotion, corporate gifts, fund-raising, or educational purposes. Special
editions can also be created to specifications. For details, contact the Special Sales
Department, Arcade Publishing, 307 West 36th Street, 11th Floor, New York,
NY 10018 or arcade@skyhorsepublishing.com.

Arcade Publishing® is a registered trademark of Skyhorse Publishing, Inc.®,
a Delaware corporation.

Visit our website at www.arcadepub.com.

10 9 8 7 6 5 4 3 2 1

Library of Congress Cataloging-in-Publication Data is available on file.
Library of Congress Control Number: 2021931112

Cover design by Erin Seaward-Hiatt
Cover illustration: © Malte Mueller/Getty Images (landscape); © GelatoPlus/
Getty Images (man's silhouette)
Author photo copyright © SUSA Argitaletxea. Used by permission.

ISBN: 978-1-951627-81-2
Ebook ISBN: 978-1-951627-95-9

Printed in the United States of America

Little brother, I will tell you my life.

This book was written with Ibrahima Balde's voice
and Amets Arzallus Antia's hand.

*With thanks to those at home
and to my friends, and to all who
helped me along the way.*

I never had time to learn to write. If you say to me, "Aminata," I know that it begins with an "a." And if you then say, "Mamadou," I think it begins with an "m." But don't ask me to spell out a whole sentence—I get confused. On the other hand, if you bring me a tool, let's say a spanner to fix a truck, I can tell you immediately, "This is a thirteen or a fourteen." If there's a jumble of spanners on the table and you cover my eyes, I'll feel one with my hand and tell you straightaway, "This is an eight."

IBRAHIMA BALDE

Ibrahima arrived in the Basque Country in October 2018. After spending a week in hospital in Bilbao with a stomach problem, he made his way to the French border between Irun and Hendaye. There, he was stopped by the French police and he remained in Irun.

I met him on the twenty-fifth of October. I think it was a Tuesday, but when I asked Ibrahima, he insisted it was a Thursday, and after working with him for a year I can confirm that his memory is much better than mine.

On that day, I was walking towards a group that helped migrants. It was a small group. We had a table in the central square of Irun where we welcomed refugees with a coffee, some conversation, a little advice.

I met Ibrahima at the entrance to the Irun train station. He was wearing a blue coat and leather sandals. I started explaining to him about our group. "*Merci*," he said.

That could mean either "Thank you," or "Yes, yes, I know all that." He told me he had now been in Irun for two days and he knew about our group. "If you want, I can help you," he said to me, "because if you want to gain the trust of migrants, it's better if they see me first and then talk to you."

We walked around Irun that morning, and I asked him where he was from. "I'm from Guinea," he answered.

"Guinea-Conakry?"

"Yes, Guinea-Conakry."

"Do you have brothers and sisters?"

He was silent for a long time and took a deep breath.

"It's not easy to describe my life," he said to me.

I realised he had a very special way of expressing himself, and also a very special wound. I suggested that we continue talking. "*Oke*," he said. And little by little, together, without noticing, we began to find the words for what is not easy to describe.

AMETS ARZALLUS ANTIA

Translator's note

The Basque Country is famous for its improvised poetry or "bertsolaritza." Bertsolaris are given themes, on which they have to improvise, publicly, in restricted verse forms. The resulting poetry has a dramatic and immediate quality to it.

The major bertsolaritza championships take place every four years. It's almost like a four-year sports tournament where dozens get eliminated before a final between the four remaining competitors. This is watched by 15,000 people in a large arena, and another 120,000 follow it on television. Out of this competition emerges a champion. One of these is Amets Arzallus Antia.

Amets himself is the child of refugees, although his parents only had to cross one border.

I grew up in the Basque Country, and return there when I can. That's where I met Amets, who gave me the book he and Ibrahima had just written, *Miñan*. I fell in love with the power of the story and the limpid quality of the language, and I asked Amets if I could translate it into English. Basque is an ancient, complex, and precise non-Indo-European language. Amets and I worked together on many aspects of the translation, but any errors are mine.

TIMBERLAKE WERTENBAKER

Part I

Part I

I

I was born in Guinea, not in Guinea-Bissau or in Equatorial Guinea. The Guinea that has as its capital Conakry. Guinea has borders with six different countries. I'll name three of them: Senegal, Sierra Leone, and Mali. Guinea is where I was born.

I am a Fula, and our language is Pulaar. But I can also speak some Malinke. I speak Susu as well. There are twenty-five different languages in Guinea. And French. That makes twenty-six. I know that because I learned it at school. But I am a Fula, and the language I know all the words of is Pulaar. I have more than a thousand words of Susu and not quite as many of Malinke. I don't know how many words of French I have.

In Susu, the word for bread is *tami* and for father *baba*. In Malinke, for mother they say *na* and for bread *dimin*. When I came into the world, my mother almost died because I was so heavy and she lost a lot of blood. The Pulaar word for blood is *yiiyan* and the word for world is *aduna*.

My birth was in Conakry because that's where my father lived, but soon after I was born, we returned to Thiankoi. Thiankoi is a village far from the sea and close to Kankalabé. The name of the region is Mamou, and it's in the prefecture of Dalaba. I lived there until I was five years old, with my mother. Father would come in March, during the rains, to help with the land that belonged to my mother. Two sisters and one brother were born after me.

We had about twelve or thirteen cows at home, and I helped my mother look after them. Sometimes my mother sent me for water, and I would go and draw it from the well. I did other work, too: I washed clothes. And I stayed close to her. Those are pretty much all the memories I have of that time with my mother. I was five years old when my father came to get me.

2

Father sold shoes. He sold them on the street, but they were house shoes, *repose-pieds*. The house is not a place for running. The place where my father sold shoes was a small table on the side of a street, about 500 metres from our house. He stayed there the whole day long. From time to time, somebody would come and they would begin to talk, first about house shoes and then about money. And then Father would be very happy. But happiness doesn't last long. After he'd spoken about money, he would take two bamboo sticks from the table and would make a small hole in each stick. My father would keep one piece, and the buyer the other. The depth of the hole measured the amount of the debt. And so Father had a lot of bamboo sticks with holes on his table. He said that one day he would leave the shoes and start to play the flute, but he continued to sell shoes.

Sometimes he went to pray and I stayed alone by the table. People came and looked at our shoes. "I can't sell them to you," I would say. "The old man isn't here, you have to wait for him." I didn't understand the complexity of money very well and I didn't know what paper bills were worth. I was very little. We would wait for the old man. The old man was my father. His name is Mamadou Bobo Balde.

I lived with my father in Conakry from the age of five until the age of thirteen. Five from thirteen is eight. But from Conakry to our little village is a little more, about four hundred and thirty *kilo*. Too far to go there on your own. And you can't walk very far in house shoes.

That's what my father would say so that I wouldn't leave. And so I stayed next to my father by the table on the side of the street. Without seeing my mother.

But I did have a friend. He was older than I was, and he loved me a lot. He always said I must ask him for anything I wanted. Sometimes I asked him for shoes, and he would bring me shoes. At other times I asked him for food, and he would bring that. I was like a little brother to him. His name was Muhtar. Once I asked him to write a letter to my mother, and he wrote it. We went together to the Conakry station, and we asked someone if they could take it all the way to my mother's village. I don't know if it went by bicycle or by bus, but I know it arrived. Distance isn't so difficult for a letter.

I think a lot about my mother. My mother is Fatimatu Diallo, and I haven't spoken to her for many months. She doesn't know I've arrived in Europe.

3

I don't like to say this, but I was afraid of my father. He would say to me: "Ibrahima, don't do that," and I wouldn't do it. But sometimes I forgot and I did it. Then father had a custom. He would ask for his belt and he would say: "Ibrahima, lie down on the floor."

"*Dakor*," I'd say, and he would give me five lashes. Or ten. I understood well why he was beating me, and I would try not to do it next time.

My father had never gone to school, and he would get angry when I didn't go. Every day, he asked me: "Ibrahima, have you gone to school today?" And I'd tell him the truth. "Yes, I've been." But sometimes, I'd have to say, "No, Father, I didn't go today, I was playing football with some friends." But before I'd even answered, Father already knew everything because I'd come in with dirty trousers. And so, when he came home from prayer in the evening, he'd say,

"Ibrahima, you know what to do." And I'd lie down on the floor and he would loosen his belt. Five lashes. Or ten. Until my back burned. Afterwards, he would put his belt back on, say a prayer, and then we'd go to bed.

I loved my father. And my father loved me.

In the morning, he was the first to get up and he'd say to me: "Ibrahima, it's time to get up." I got up, said my prayers, and went to school.

School wasn't always easy, because they only taught French. French and three other things. First, how to cross the street. You look to the left, then to the right, and then you cross. Second, they taught us to respect people. You have to respect people because . . . that's the way it is. Third . . . I've forgotten. I can't remember, but I think it was very important. Those are the three things I learned at school.

It was a state school, but I left before I'd completed year seven. I had no means of support. Means—that is, money, and money is always necessary. I wanted to continue school, but it wasn't possible.

4

Our father was a good man, but he had a disease, diabetes. At times, we had to go to the hospital, and when we were at the hospital we couldn't be at the table selling shoes.

And that meant that our sales went down, and then we found ourselves without money.

Father asked me some hard questions: "Ibrahima, how will we manage now? My health is not good and you're still a child."

I answered: "I'll leave school, Father, and I'll look for a way to make money."

But he didn't want this, and he always answered: "You're too little. For you, it's still morning. You'll do all that later." But later doesn't always come.

One afternoon at sixteen zero zero, I returned home from school. I went into the house, washed a little, and went out into the street to my father's table. But that day father wasn't himself. "I'm cold," he said to me.

"*Dakor*," I answered, "I'll go home and get you a jacket. Wait here for a few minutes."

"Hurry up," he said.

I brought a jacket and a chair for him to sit on. I started to organise the merchandise, but that day Father was not himself.

We went home and he asked if I was hungry. "No, I'm all right," I said.

"I'm going to the mosque to pray, and then I'll come home," he said.

"*Dakor*," I said, "I'll wait for you here."

When he came home, he asked if I'd recited my prayers and I said yes, but it was a lie.

PART I

Even now, I remember that lie. I didn't want to tell him the truth, because it was such a sad truth. While he was at the mosque, I was thinking: *If I ever find myself without my father, my life will be at an end. He's the only one who can help me by paying a little money for me to go to school.* That's what I kept thinking, but I didn't tell him. We said a prayer together and we went to bed. It was twenty-one zero zero.

At twenty-three zero zero, Father got up again. I wasn't asleep. "I have a terrible headache," he said. He gave me a thousand-franc note and sent me to buy him some medicine. "Ask for paracetamol," he told me. I went into the street, but everything was dark and all the pharmacies were closed. I walked almost three *kilo* trying to find one that was open, but it was no good. I returned all the way home without the paracetamol. "It doesn't matter," Father said to me. "It will pass." But I touched his body and it was burning. We stayed together, next to each other, for a little while. And then I went to sleep.

I woke up at six, and I noticed Father was still sleeping. "Father," I said, "it's already day. You're usually up by now, but today you haven't got up." He didn't answer me. I repeated this three times, and still he didn't answer. I tapped my fingers on his bed a little to see if he would get up, but he didn't move. I put my hand under his chin, and it was like touching ice. I touched his whole body. It was all frozen. "Father," I started again, "it's already morning, you're usually up by now, but today you haven't got up." He didn't answer me, and I began to feel frightened.

With something like this, I didn't know what had to be done. I ran out of the house shouting: "*Faabo, faabo.*" That means "I need help"in our language. The neighbours came out.

"Ibrahima, what's happened?"they asked me.

"Father is having some difficulties," I said. "Come in and you'll see for yourselves."

The neighbours called other neighbours, and those neighbours called others. Before I knew it, there was all this commotion in our house. Finally, someone went to find the imam. When he came, he looked first at my father and then at me. Then he looked at my father again and came up to me.

"Ibrahima," he said, "you must now come with me."

"I can't," I said. "I have to stay here."

The imam was insistent.

"No, Ibrahima, you must come with me. It's not possible for you to stay here."

"I don't care," I said. "Whatever has happened, I'm staying here with my father."

I thought they were hiding something from me, and I said to them: "I went out of the house to ask for help. If something has happened to Father, I believe I have to know what the problem is."

And then they told me that my father was no longer alive.

5

Now I know that when someone is dying they begin to freeze. Or perhaps they freeze first and then they die. I'm not sure about that. I wanted to go to my mother and explain this, and also to ask her for some advice. For example: "Mother, what am I going to do with my life now?"

I had an old uncle in Conakry. He was an older brother of my father's, and I went to him. I told him that Father was dead and that I wanted to go and find my mother in her village, but he told me he didn't have any money. "*Oke*," I answered. And I went back home.

Our home consisted of just one room. There wasn't a kitchen. There was a small praying corner and a bed. I slept on the floor, on a rug.

Father paid a hundred thousand Guinean francs a month to rent our home. A hundred thousand Guinean francs is ten euros. Yes, ten euros. When I say it like that it sounds simple, but for me it wasn't simple at all. How could I pay that sum for the house? And how could I pay for the bus that would take me to my mother's house? I sat on the stairs and I thought of those two things, especially the second one. There was a third thing as well and I couldn't wave it away: my father and his frozen body. And at that moment, I began to cry.

In the end, a neighbour came to me. And then another. And then more. They weren't rich—we all lived in a big block in *"the haute banlieue de Conakry"*—but they had kind hearts. They patted me on the head and they soon raised enough money among themselves for me to go to my mother.

"Jaarama buy," I said to them. In our language, *Jaarama buy* means "Thank you."

"It's nothing," they said to me and then, "Good luck."

I took a deep breath, as if to hold on to this luck, and I went out into the street.

6

Conakry station is very big. We call it the *"gare voitures"* or the *"gare voitures de Bambetto."* The buses going to our village leave on Mondays and Thursdays at six in the afternoon. But they don't go all the way; they stop at Kankalabé. To get to Thiankoi you have to go on foot—it's about nine *kilo*. I left Conakry on a Thursday afternoon and arrived in Thiankoi on Friday evening. It was dark.

When I went into the house, I didn't manage to say anything, but as soon as my mother looked at me, she guessed something was wrong.

"Ibrahima, what's happened to you?" she asked.

"I'm not very well, Mother," I said, and then I was silent. We remained like that, looking at each other.

And then,: "Ibrahima, I think there is something you are hiding from me," she said.

She took a chair and sat next to me. We started to speak. About father's diabetes and then about school, what I was learning. "Ibrahima, if father has lost his life, I want to know," she said.

"Of course," I said, and then she understood everything. She started crying, lamenting, and she talked about my father's life. I regretted a little what I'd done, I hadn't wanted to tell her that very night that father had died. I knew she would cry a lot and wake up everyone in the house. But I hadn't been able to keep back my words. And so we stayed like that until dawn, each in a chair, next to each other, close.

The first to wake up in the morning were my two little sisters, Fatumata Binta and Rouguiatou. And then my little brother, Alhassane, woke up. When I saw them, all my courage left me. I realised we were in a house without hope. And I was the eldest. I don't know if you understand what that means.

My mother was looking at an old photograph of my father. "Father," I said. But he didn't answer. "Mother," I said to her a little afterwards, "now I won't be able to continue studying." But she didn't answer either.

13

7

Our mother has a lot of patience, but she doesn't have much strength. When I say strength, I mean ability, and by ability I mean the ability to make money. Mother has a small parcel of land, which she cultivates. She has a few cows and some goats and a little vegetable garden. Nothing more.

When I told her that father was dead, she said to me: "Ibrahima, I am going to sell two cows. You'll be able to start something with what I get for them." I told her not to do that, that our home needed the cows more, there were three other children behind me and they also had to be looked after, but she didn't pay attention.

Three days later, she came to me. "Ibrahima, here is the money." Nine hundred thousand Guinean *frankos*. Nine hundred thousand Guinean *frankos* are ninety euros. "This money is here to make more money," she insisted, and I knew then what I had to say to her.

"Mother, I don't have any experience of business," I explained. "And I've already thought about all this a little. I think the best is for me to go somewhere else—there aren't any opportunities here."

She held her head with both her hands and she started to cry. She asked if I wanted to escape from the house.

"No, Mother, no, that's not it at all."

In the end, she began to have confidence in my words. "*Oke*," she said. "'*Oke*," and then she said two other things. First: "Ibrahima, take good care of yourself." And second: "Every day I will pray to God to look after you."

"*Jaarama buy*," I answered. And I left for Conakry.

8

Many buses leave from the Conakry bus station, going in all directions. I was sitting on a bench, watching all this movement. *I'll go to Liberia*, I told myself. I'm not sure why: maybe because of the name; it was an easy name to pronounce. Sierra Leone was further away, and so was the Ivory Coast. And someone had told me it was easier for a child to find some kind of work in Liberia. I think that's what made me decide, even though I was no longer a child: I was thirteen.

There was a minibus with L.I.B.E.R.I.A written on the front of the windscreen, but when I approached the driver, he shook his head: "I can't take you," he said. "You're too young."

"I'm thirteen," I told him.

"That's right, too young," he said.

I began to insist a little, and he asked me if I had any family in Liberia. I told him I didn't. "Then why do you want to go there?" he asked.

"How much time do you have?" I answered.

He told me the bus would leave in twenty-eight minutes.

"*Oke*," I said, and I explained my situation to him.

He listened carefully to everything I said. "I'll take you," he agreed, "but you'll have to go on the roof, next to the luggage."

"Thank you," I answered, and I climbed on the minibus roof. In Africa, it's not like here—all the luggage is piled on top of the buses.

I placed myself in the middle of all the suitcases and sat with my legs dangling down over the side. The trip took a long time, three whole days. My bottom was a little sore and my head felt hot. During those three days, I thought about a lot of things. One, why I had decided to go to Liberia. Two, what I was going to do once I arrived there. Three, in what state I had left Mother, Alhassane, Fatumata Binta, and Rouguiatou at home. And four, when were we going to get there?

The bus began to slow down at dawn. "Monrovia," someone cried, and all the people got off. Afterwards, the driver climbed up onto the minibus roof rack and threw down their luggage.

"You have to get off here as well," he said.

"*Oke*," I answered, and I jumped down onto the ground.

9

In Liberia, many words change, especially the sound of words. People use a different language there: I learned the word *market*. And in Monrovia, the market is very large. It's called Watazai. To turn it into a French word, I think you have to lengthen the sound of the *a* somewhat so that it sounds like *Watazaaai*. In English, they just call it Waterside, a town near the water.

Watazai market is so immense my eyes couldn't take it all in at once. There's a strange mixture of smells, and people carry large and heavy loads on foot, sometimes more than they can manage. I started to help these people. Whenever I saw someone carrying a load too heavy for them, I took it from them and walked with them. Then they would pay me something: three *libati*, seven *libati*, or fifteen *libati*. And in that way, little by little, I started to earn some money.

When you're thirteen, it's not easy work to carry heavy loads. I was still very little, whereas the boxes I was carrying were already very big. There were boxes full of fruit, sometimes they were full of pineapples, and at other times avocados. Or sometimes clothes. And there were some boxes, I don't know what was in them, but I didn't have the strength to carry them. "I can't," I would say to the people, "this box is tougher than I am."

"*Oke*," they said. "We'll ask someone else to carry it." And then they wouldn't give me any money.

In the end, the people from Watazai started to trust me and they would call out my name. "Ibrahima, come here and help me carry this package." "Ibrahima, here's some money for you." This is very important for me, to experience closeness. But at night, all the people I knew were gone, and I remained alone. I would go back to the bus station and place some cardboard on the floor to make myself a small bed. It was there, in Liberia, that I learned to sleep on the streets.

I lived like that for three months, working in the market and sleeping in the station. In the end, I began to lose my sense of time. So that I don't know exactly when what I'm about to describe to you happened. But I know it was a weekend, maybe a Saturday or a Sunday.

I saw a man in a garage: he was working on a machine, and his hands were dirty. I was looking at him, and he was looking at me.

"Are you Guinean?" he asked me.

"Yes."

"Then we're two," he said. He turned his back to me and continued working. Two minutes went by. Maybe three. He turned back again to look at me.

"Why have you come to Liberia?" he asked.

"I came here to plan my future."

"Do you have parents here?"

"No."

"Do you have any work?"

"I help people in the market by carrying loads for them."

"And you think that's the way to plan your future?"

"No, but I don't have any other choice."

He was silent again, and we stayed like that for a long time as I continued to watch him and he continued to work.

"I'd like some other work too," I ventured. He didn't answer me. He was fixing the motor of a truck. He finished what he was doing, and lifted his head.

"What kind of work would you like to do?"

"I'd like to drive a truck. Ever since I was a child I've loved big trucks, and since then I've always watched very carefully how people drive them." I said all of this to him without stopping.

"I drive a truck," he said, "but you're too young to become an apprentice. How old are you?"

"Thirteen."

"You're too young."

"I know, but I'm growing up, and I could do something— you can ask me to do anything and I'll do it." I repeated this twice, maybe three times, and he told me to wait, as he wanted a little time to think about it. "*Oke,*" I answered. And I returned to the market.

10

I spent three days carrying boxes full of fruit. My shoulders were hurting. It was Tuesday or maybe Wednesday, I'm not sure now. The man I had met in the garage came to the market, but I didn't see him. I was carrying a very large load. He was walking behind me, but I didn't notice him. As I was putting down my load, he said my name, "Ibrahima." I turned around.

"Have you had lunch?" he asked.

"No," I answered, and he took me to an eating place nearby. He asked for a little bit of rice for both of us. We sat facing each other, and we ate from the same bowl.

"Ibrahima," he said, "I don't want to see you do that work anymore, it's too heavy for you."

"I know," I said, "but I have no other choice—that's why I do it."

"If you want, you can come with me. I'll take you on as my apprentice."

That sentence was the very first work contract I had in my life.

Tanba Tegiano was the man's name, and Behn was his truck's name. Behn was a very big truck and I was too small to drive it, but I did many other things. I changed the oil, I put air into the tyres, and I helped attach the cargo. When I couldn't attach the cargo, I would sit on top of it. "That way it won't move so much," Tanba would say.

I worked as an apprentice for six months, and I understood a lot about the habits of trucks. About people as well. For example, Tanba wasn't a Muslim: he didn't read the verses of the Koran, he didn't pray five times a day. He was with another team, with the Catholics, and the Catholics had other habits and used different tactics. Tanba explained all this to me. And I said: "That's fine, Tanba, your Behn is a very big truck and a lot of people can fit inside it."

Tanba was a good man. I don't know how I can thank him for everything he did for me. He fed me, he clothed me, he took me into his family. I lived for six months in their house, with his wife and his two children, all together four other people. I was the fifth. They slept in the bedroom, and I slept in the sitting room, on a rug.

One day, I called home.

Mother answered: "*Allo?*" I asked her how she was, and she answered: "*Jam tun.*" In Pulaar, "*jam tun*" means fine. But afterwards my younger brother took the telephone, and he didn't say, "*Jam tun.*"

"Ibrahima, Mother is not well. She's having some difficulties with her health. I don't understand it all, but I'm worried. If you can come home, you should."

"*Oke,*" I answered, and I put the telephone down. I felt frozen. I had to say something to Tanba.

"Tanba, my mother isn't feeling well, I want to ask your permission to go back to Guinea."

"Ibrahima, you're just starting to understand the world of big trucks, and you want to leave now?"

"No, it's not like that," I explained. "I want to stay here, but my mother is ill and I have to go back. Alhassane has asked me to."

Tanba was silent and then he said, "I know." But I didn't understand what he knew.

"If you want, we'll call again," I urged him. "You can speak with my mother or with my brother, Alhassane, and you'll understand my reasons better."

Tanba was silent again and then he said, "I know, I understand. And if you have to go, I'll help you."

He gave me a big pack full of things. And a little money. I carried the money in my pocket and the big pack on my back, and I returned to Conakry. I went straight from Conakry to Kankalabé by bus. And from there, I went to Thiankoi on foot.

I I

When I returned home, I found my mother in a very fragile state.

"I'll take you to the hospital," I said.

"To the hospital—how?" she asked me.

"Don't you worry, Mother, I know what to do."

Do you know how I took her to the hospital? I carried her on my back, piggyback.

From our house to the hospital is nine *kilo*, almost ten. We went the whole way on foot, and each step was an exploit for both of us. Tired, bent forward, I would put mother on the ground and take a break. Later, I'd go down on all fours and say to her: "Climb up." She'd hold on to my back, and on we went. My little brother walked next to me. "There isn't that far to go," he said sometimes. At least seven times, he said, "There isn't that far to go." In the end, we got there.

At the hospital, we waited three or four hours in the waiting room. At last the doctor came and told us that Mother had liquid blocked in her whole body. "At least two litres of water," he explained to us. He prescribed some medicines. "And now you can go," he told us.

"Our house is very far away," I explained to him.

"*Oke*," he agreed. "I'll take your mother on my motorbike, but you two will have to return on foot.

"*Dakor*," we both answered, Alhassane and I.

We made the return trip talking. Talking and on foot. We were lighter and faster.

First in her womb, nine months or more. Then on her breast or on her back, how many more years? Washing you, feeding you as you're growing. And so, we Fulás of Guinea have a saying, and it goes like this:

23

Even if you take your mother on your back
And carry her on foot all the way to Mecca
You still will not have paid a single penny
Of what you owe for all that she has done for you.

12

If I'd had the choice, I wouldn't have wanted to be the oldest son. Maybe the second son or the last one, but not the oldest. That would have changed a few things. But God decided otherwise, and there was nothing I could do to change it. In our house, I was in first position, and in second position was Alhassane.

When I returned from Liberia, Alhassane was still a child, but he was beginning to understand things. It seemed to me that he had grown up a lot during the time I'd been away. When you're the oldest in a household, that often happens: responsibility makes your body grow. And all his teachers said: "That child understands things very quickly."

On the day we took my mother to the hospital, he asked me, "*Koto*, what are you going to do now?" *Koto* in our language means "older brother."

"While Mother is ill, I'll stay in the house," I answered, "I won't go back to Liberia."

Alhassane didn't say anything, but he was very happy. He laughed. With his mouth. And with his eyes.

Alhassane left the house very early in the morning because his school was a long way away. About nine *kilo*. And his steps were small, because he was only eleven years old. One day, I brought him an old bicycle so that he could make the journey there and back much faster. As soon as he came home, if he knew I was washing clothes near the well, he would come and place himself next to me and, without asking for anything, start to help me.

Alhassane knew what the situation was in our house. And he never asked for anything. Sometimes I would sense that there was something he wanted—perhaps new shoes, or some nice clothes, so that he could look more like his classmates. But he never asked. He knew we couldn't have these things. I could read everything in his eyes, and I tried to bring him what I could so that he would feel happy about going to school. Father had once said to me: "Ibrahima, you must try to do everything you can so that Alhassane can continue learning in school."

I often remember that particular sentence now.

13

In the end, I spent two years at home. Often, Mother woke up feeling very weak and had to lie in the hammock. And so I turned into a mother. I went to fetch water from the well, and I carried wood. Then I looked after the cows, and I washed out the bowls of the little ones. Housework is like that. In most houses, it's the mother who does the housework, but in our house I did it.

There was one aspect of that work I really enjoyed. And that was when I carried my little sisters on my back. To do that you have to make knots in a sheet. You don't see much of that here, but in Africa everyone knows how to make these knots that go around the neck. It's a little complicated, but if you try once or twice, by the third time you know how to do it. The important thing is to have a long sheet.

I have two little sisters, Fatumata Binta and Rouguiatou. I think I told you that at the beginning. Rouguiatou is the smallest, and it's pronounced like this: Rou-gui-a-tou. Fatumata Binta is a little older, three or four years, and pronouncing it is more difficult because it's a longer name. But you don't really pronounce Fatumata—you swallow that name and just use Binta.

My little sisters had never gone to school, but when we last spoke on the phone, Binta told me she wanted to start to learn something.

"Of course," I answered. "Now that you're growing up, you must go to school and then learn a profession."

"Like what?" she asked.

"You could learn to sew or embroider. Would you like that?"

26

She said she would. And then she passed the phone to Rouguiatou, who asked me if I thought that one day we would see each other again. And I said, "Inshallah, I would like that very much." And she said that she remembered me every day, and that once she started thinking about me, she could never stop.

"And why do you think about me and not about Alhassane?" I asked.

"I can't answer that, *Koto*, but I think that you and Mother are hiding some things from me."

Rouguiatou is now eleven years old. Maybe even twelve. I'm not sure.

14

I stayed in Thiankoi until I was sixteen years old, looking after the cows and goats, and washing the clothes of my little sisters. Alhassane also helped me a lot. Sometimes, we would stop working for a little time and each sit on a chair, and we would talk. "Life isn't easy," one of us would say. "No, no, it isn't easy," the other would agree. And we started to make plans for the future.

"Alhassane, you must continue to study. Your eyes are very big, and with those you'll learn many things." I wanted to say that he was a bright and lively boy, but I don't know if he really understood. I began to notice that his wishes were changing.

One day, he said to me: "*Koto*, I want to start helping you."

"How can you help me?" I asked.

"I want a job."

"What job?"

"I don't know."

And he remained silent, pensive. He didn't know what to say. "Maybe I could be a motorbike mechanic," he suggested.

"No, Alhassane, you're still too young, you're not even fourteen, you have to stay in school and continue to learn."

"*Oke*," he answered.

He didn't dare contradict me, but his ideas were most definitely changing. He didn't want to stay in school, and he was ready to go anywhere. "Alhassane, let's take a walk," I suggested to him. And I began to tell him about my life. How from the age of five to the age of thirteen I lived in Conakry, staying by Father's table on the side of the street. And then I told him about my six months in Liberia with Tanba's truck. Just as I'm telling you everything now.

"I know all that," he said to me.

Little by little, Mother started to become stronger, and this changed my situation. And so, one evening, I went to her and said: "Forgive me, Mother."

"What is it?" she asked. "What's wrong?"

"I've been thinking a little, and I'm going back to Conakry. I want to see what is happening there." Mother was silent and lowered her head.

"Yes, Mother, I'm hopeful that in Conakry I can earn a little money. Otherwise Alhassane will leave school."

When I said this, Mother began to cry, and she gave me a kiss on my forehead.

The next day, early in the morning, I left for Conakry.

15

Nzérékoré is the name of a Guinean city, and the round-trip journey from there to Conakry is about 1,300 *kilo* by road. I made that journey for three or four years, in a truck, having been accepted as something like an apprentice by a truck driver. One week, we went from Conakry to Nzérékoré, and the following week, we returned from Nzérékoré to Conakry. This driver did a lot for me and taught me a profession.

I remember one night when we were going towards Banankoro, up a mountain. There was a very heavy load on the truck, and it was in trouble. I was aware of this, but I kept quiet and tried to will the truck to keep going. And then, suddenly, *ka-ka-ka-ka-ka*—we heard a loud noise. The boss told me to get out at once and find out where the noise was coming from. I jumped out. "Put it into first gear and go

29

forward slowly," I told him. He did that. But then, *ka-ka-ka-ka-ka*—that same grinding noise.

"The noise is coming from under the axle," I told him.

"It's the drive shaft," he said. "The drive shaft is wrecked."

We left the truck and placed ourselves in the middle of the road to see if anything was coming. Twenty minutes, forty minutes, a whole hour. The only thing that passed was time. In the end, a motorbike came in the middle of the night, and we motioned for it to stop. The boss went to Banankoro to look for a new drive shaft. I stayed inside the truck, on the side of the road.

At the end of two days, the boss came back.

Now I can tell the difference between a problem with a truck's motor and a problem with the body parts. I understand what a motor is saying very well and what other mechanical parts are saying as well. But if there's an electrical problem, I don't know what to do. I can drive a little, too. Sometimes the boss would let me drive for a bit—three or four *kilo* when the truck was empty and when there weren't too many bends in the road. "Ibrahima, bring me a large can," he would say, and I'd bring him a ten-litre can. He would settle himself on the passenger seat and say to me: "Off you go." And I would sit on top of the can with my hands on the wheel.

That's how I learned to drive.

16

One day, while we were in Nzérékoré, the boss handed me his phone so that I could call home. It had been some time since I'd known what was happening in Thiankoi. There was a noise, and then I heard my mother's voice.

"*Allo?*"

"Mother, it's Ibrahima. How are you?"

"*Jam tun, alhamdoulillah*, and you?"

"I'm well, too, praise be to God."

After those two or three customary sentences, I asked again, "Mother, are you well?"

"Yes, I'm well," she said, "but for the last three weeks we haven't had any news of Alhassane. He left the house one day, and I haven't heard anything from him since. Do you know anything, Ibrahima?"

I didn't know anything. It was now three or four years since I'd moved far away from home, and during all that time I had only spoken to Alhassane three times. He had never expressed to me any desire to go anywhere.

"Give me a little time," I said to my mother, "I'll try to find out something."

When I got back to Conakry, I went to my father's older brother and I asked if he knew whether by any chance Alhassane had come there. He answered no, he didn't know anything. "*Oke*," I said. And I returned to the garage.

Time passed, maybe a couple of weeks, perhaps a month or even more, without any news of Alhassane. I decided to go back to the village, to my mother.

I bought two bags of rice in Conakry and took the bus to Kankalabé. From there, I went to Thiankoi on foot, with the bags of rice on my back. I found my mother outside the house, in the vegetable patch.

"Ibrahima," she said to me.

"Mother," I answered, "I didn't know anything about this."

I stayed home for a week, and Alhassane's absence forced me to begin to confront my own weakness. When I say weakness, what I really want to say is guilt. Yes, my guilt. Because I had talked about helping him stay in school and keep learning, but I hadn't been able to do that. I was only an apprentice—I hadn't earned any money. And now he'd gone away.

In front of the house, there was an orange tree, which my father had planted. I sat next to it and I thought: *Where could my little brother possibly have gone?* Binta and Rouguiatou came close, but I didn't pay any attention to them. I couldn't. I wanted to go. To Liberia, to Mali, to Sierra Leone, Mauritania—somewhere where I could find traces of my little brother.

I asked my mother many questions to find out what she thought.

"Ibrahima," she said to me, "you must return to Conakry. Don't leave your apprenticeship. As soon as I have some news, I'll get in touch with you."

"*Dakor,*" I answered, and I returned to Conakry.

I was learning to carry a heavy load.

I 7

Several months passed without us knowing anything. And then, one day, a friend came to find me in the garage. It was Friday, the day we changed the filters of the truck and put in new oil. "Ibrahima," he said to me, and I turned my head around. "Your mother called me, there's some news of Alhassane."

"*Ah, bon?*"

"Yes, Alhassane is in Libya." I remained silent. He said it again: "Alhassane is in Libya."

I took in a breath. I felt a constriction in my throat. *He's a child. The last time I saw him he wasn't even fourteen—what has he gone looking for in Libya? And how could he decide to go there without telling me anything? That's not how the two of us agreed to do things.* That's what I thought. And something else: *How did he get to Libya without any money?*

That afternoon, I called my mother.

"Mother, who told you Alhassane was in Libya?"

"Ibrahima, I spoke with him, and he's the one who told me."

"And are you sure you understood everything?" When I asked my mother that, she became a little angry.

"Ibrahima, are you aware that you are doubting the words of your own mother?"

"Of course I'm not," I answered.

But I wasn't sure, because I don't think my mother had ever looked at a map of Africa and realised that Libya was a long way away. You could say to her, "Here is Libya, there's Algeria, and that's Morocco," and Mother would answer "*Oke*," but without knowing what that meant.

"Ibrahima, Alhassane is in Libya," she said again. And she gave me a telephone number. "Alhassane called from that number. You call him and try to speak to him."

"*Dakor*," I answered her.

After I'd hung up, *He's in Libya*, I thought. *Libya*.

18

Three times, I tried to call the number my mother had given me. No one answered.

The fourth time, yes.

"*Allo?*" said an old man.

Me: "Alhassane?"

And the old man's voice: "Wait." I heard him call out: "Alhassane Balde? Alhassane Balde?"

Shortly afterwards, Alhassane took the phone. As soon as we started to speak, the child started to cry.

"*Miñan*, what have you gone to look for in Libya?" I asked him. *Miñan* is a Pulaar word, and it means "little brother or sister"—we say it to the younger children of the family.

He answered that he wanted to go to Europe.

"And you were going to go to Europe without saying anything to me?"

He asked me to forgive him. He wanted to help me, but he didn't know how.

"*Miñan*," I said to him, "only God can help us, no one else."

"I know," he said. And then he spoke at length.

"I'm only asking you for one thing, *Koto*: don't forget Mother. Don't think about anything else. Don't think about how I left the house. Don't think about how I left school. I want to follow a path that will help us all, because back there, we have no way forward. I looked. There isn't any future."

"I know, *miñan*," I answered. "I know all of that."

My phone credit was quickly running out, and I asked him where he was. He said he was in Sabratha, in a large refugee camp called Baba Hassan, where they were waiting for the opportunity to cross the sea.

"Be careful, *miñan*," I urged him.

Yes, he said, he would be careful. He was giving me his word.

Three or four days later, I started the journey to find my brother. I got on a minibus that was going from Conakry to Siguiri. It was ten zero zero.

Part II

Part II

I

I arrived in Siguiri the following afternoon, at sixteen zero zero hours. I stayed there until dark, thinking: *I want to go to Bamako, but it's not cheap, even though mother sold three goats.* I walked around, asking people where they were going, and at last I saw the driver of a truck.

"Where are you going?" I asked him.

"To Bamako," he answered. "Every fortnight I do the return trip from Conakry to Bamako."

"I've often travelled in a truck," I told him. "I know how to go places without disturbing the driver."

He was silent, looking at me. He studied my face, my body, my bag. "How much money do you have?"

"Not much."

"If you give me thirty-three thousand Guinean *franko*, I'll take you."

"*Oke*," I said.

He opened the back. "Get in," he said. I made the whole trip in the back of the truck, hiding in a large pile of wheat.

Bamako is at a crossroads. A lot of roads come into it, and many others leave from it. Roads, people, and merchandise.

No one ever stays there for long. At the station, I heard them speak in Susu, and I thought, *There are some Guineans here*. I asked one of them: "Are you by any chance going from here to Gao?"

"No," he answered. "The station where they have buses going to Gao isn't here. This station is for Guinea. The station for Gao is over there."

"I don't know Bamako at all," I told him.

"Then follow me," he said.

We started crossing Bamako. First we went right, then we went left, and from there, I don't know which way we went. I can't remember now. But we got there.

The Gao station is very big. There were a lot of people there. Some were sleeping on benches; others were drinking coffee. Some were carrying children on their backs; others were just milling about. I went up to the ticket desk, and I asked, "How much is the bus to Gao?"

"From Bamako to Gao costs nine thousand *franko*," answered the ticket vendor.

The money in Mali is also *franko*, but it's called CFA as well, and it's not worth the same as the Guinean *franko*. In Mali, nine thousand *franko* is more or less thirteen euros.

"*Oke*," I said to the vendor, and he gave me a ticket.

It was dark during the trip, and the whole bus was asleep. When I woke up, it was the desert.

2

The road to Gao is long. And it is not easy. The heat burns the window. The window burns the ears. The bus doesn't stop. Even while you're asleep, the bus keeps going. It goes far. After a night, even further.

Two nights. And then three. And then Gao.

The bus stopped by a bridge, and we were told to get out. On one side of the river, there were soldiers from Mali, and on the other side, Tuaregs. I noticed that on both sides they were carrying guns. Each group was watching its side of the river as if they were in a war against each other. But as we got off the bus, they signalled to us at the same time, and their movements were coordinated.

Yes. That's because they were directing the traffic together: the traffic of migrants.

The bus left me at the entrance of the bridge next to the Mali soldiers, but I couldn't step onto the bridge. "Stop," ordered a soldier. "Stay where you are." From the other side of the bridge, a Tuareg with a pickup truck came to find me and took me to it. The Malian soldier looked on and didn't say a thing.

We were nine people in the pickup truck. During the journey, an armed man walked up and down and asked: "Musa Onze or Musa Kone?" Musa Onze is a warlord, and Musa Kone is another warlord, and between them they control all of Northern Mali. I know all this now, but I didn't know anything then—it was the first time I had heard those names.

"I don't have any contacts with anyone here," I said.

"You want to go to Algeria?" they asked me.

And I answered, "*Oui*."

But they didn't take me there.

The pickup truck stopped by a very high wall. Halfway along the wall, there was a small door that opened from the bottom upwards, and they pushed me in. "*Allez*. Go in there." Inside was an enclosure, with walls and wire. And inside the walls were people, a lot of people, imprisoned. I don't know how many we were—a hundred and twenty, a hundred and forty, I don't know. When there are a lot of people, it's hard to count exactly, but there were a lot of us there. And all of them were like me.

The guards were asking for money. "Pay up and you'll go to Algeria." And then they raised their guns. "And if you don't pay up, we'll shoot you." Those who were doing these things weren't children. They were my age. They were old enough to know what they were doing. But they still did it.

I took out my mother's three goats" worth: seven hundred thousand Guinean *franko*, or seventy euros.

"Don't you have any more?"

"No."

They wrote my name on a list and, some days later, a truck came to get us.

3

Ninety-four people got onto the truck, that's one hundred minus six. And then everyone got down in Kidal, and they counted us again: "Forty, sixty, eighty, fourteen more, ninety-four, *c'est oke*."

And we set off again, into the desert's vastness.

Here, you have the sea; but there, we have the desert. If you have never seen the desert with your own eyes, you cannot really understand what it is like. The desert is another world. When you go into it, you think: *I will never get out of here*.

There, the people all look the same. They all speak Arabic, or Tuareg, or they say they are Tuaregs but they speak Arabic. I don't know the difference between them. I believe they all belong to Boko Haram or to the Islamic State. But I don't really know.

We stayed in the truck for five days, without any food. We had a little tin of drinking water—nothing else. Some people threw up, others did their business in their trousers. There, if you wanted to have a pee, you had to do it in your trousers— you had no choice. Because the truck never stopped.

I thought I was going to Algeria, because that is what they had told me in Gao. Others said they wanted to go to Italy, and went onto a truck for Italy. Most people chose Spain, and they climbed onto a truck for Spain. But it was all a lie, a game to take away our money.

4

When you fall into the hands of the Tuaregs, you can't move forwards, you can't move backwards; you're stuck in the middle, in the middle of nowhere. And at that moment, you see a prison, in the heart of the desert. A prison that is run by adults and children. And there, all of them have a Kalashnikov slung over their shoulder. You ask, "Where am I?" You are in Taalanda.

A big door marks the entrance. I went in that one without having to bend my head, and I found myself in a large wasteland that appeared heavily fortified. At regular intervals, there were narrow little huts, putt, putt, putt, arranged neatly, like shoeboxes. In each enclosure, an armed person or two. But wait—Taalanda doesn't end there. In the middle of a large wall, there was another passage, and that passage led into another space, circular and covered in sand. Empty in the middle and all around, high walls. They took me there. Do you know what that place is? It's a market, a market where they sell people.

I'll tell you how it works.

You're in your corner, sitting on the ground or maybe lying down. The ground is sandy. Every day, they come by with a large pot. You have to hold out your arm and spread out your hand. And then they throw the food at you. As if you were a dog. But sometimes the food they bring is so hot that it burns your hand. And so you let it drop on the floor, and then you remain without food. Tomorrow, they'll come again, in the same way, at the same time. But I think I wanted to say something else to you—I've lost the thread. Where was I?

Ah yes, the market, the market of Taalanda. Let me start again.

You are in your corner, lying on the ground, or maybe sitting. The ground is sandy. Somebody says your name, or without bothering with a name, calls out: "*Toi, viens ici*. You, come here." And then you have to go and place yourself in the centre. The person who is interested in buying comes in and starts to look at you. Up and down. Down and up. Then: "*Oke*," he'll say.

They call someone else. The buyer looks at that one up and down, down and up. The way he looked at you. And when the inspection is finished, "I want that one and that one," he says. The Tuareg proposes a price, and again the buyer looks at you. Up and down. Down and up. And he gives the money to the Tuareg.

*

But they didn't buy me. They came and looked at me, once, twice, three times, but they didn't take me. And so I stayed there. For three days. In Taalanda.

5

There are only two ways to get out of Taalanda. One is if someone buys you and takes you away. You don't know where to, you don't know what for. The other possibility is for your family to send money. But for that to happen, the family has to have money in the first place.

When I entered the prison, they searched every part of my body. When I talk about every part of my body, I mean all the holes of my body as well. And all my clothes too. That's how they find out if you have any money on you. But I wasn't carrying anything—only an identity card in a pocket, nothing else. They took that away. That's why I have no papers, and without papers you're worth less than a goat. Even so, the Tuaregs ordered me to call my family and to ask them for money. "Otherwise, we'll kill you."

I didn't call anyone. And I stayed there, a prisoner. Every day, food fit for a dog. And the looks. Up and down. Down and up. And after that, "*Oke*."

But there is one other way out of Taalanda, the last possibility. *La fugue.* To escape. That's what I did, and I'll tell you how. But wait a little, I need to drink a sip of water.

And so, now, yes, *la fugue*.

In Taalanda, I made friends with another prisoner. He was Guinean, a Susu. I can speak more than a thousand words of Susu. The Tuaregs, not one. On the third day, I approached him and I said, "*Boore*, tonight we can make our escape." *Boore* is a Susu word, and it means "friend."

"Yes," he said, "I want to escape as well, but how? These walls are high, much higher than we are." He'd begun to despair.

"They're high, but they're a little worn," I told him. "There are holes in them, and it may be that we can climb up these walls."

"*Oke*, we'll see," he answered.

And we waited for the night to come.

At night, in the dark, we did as we had planned. They were all sleeping: the prisoners, the guards, the walls. We got up and confronted the high walls. But there were holes in the walls, at least twenty holes. "You follow me," I said to my friend, and I started climbing up, carefully. One, spot the hole. Two, place the hand in the hole. Three, pull up the whole body. And in that way, hole by hole, I climbed to the top of the wall, like a very little ant.

From the top, I jumped down, to the other side.

But the other side was still Taalanda. A circular courtyard surrounded us, and another wall stood between us and our escape. It was at least six or seven metres high.

I scanned it with my eyes to see if there was a way to climb it, using some holes in that wall. One there on the left, one to the right, maybe. In the end, I found a very long piece of wood, and placed it against the wall to use as a kind of ladder or slide. Arms, stomach, feet, all this without ever letting out a sound. I used all the strength I had, and eventually managed to pull myself to the top of the wall. My skin was scraped, my heart compressed. And then I slid down the other side, six or seven metres at least.

On the other side, it was all sand. And sand knows how to remain silent.

My friend also managed to get to the top of the wall, but once at the top, he leaned over too much and he fell. He remained there, lying on the sand, unable to get up. He was screaming, "Aaaaaahhhhhh." I think he had broken a bone, but I'm not sure, I don't know. I didn't help him. I was running. Escaping. I didn't know where to, but escaping.

I heard cries behind me, and I kept going, running.

After I'd covered a little distance, I stopped, lay down on the sand, and looked back. I saw a light, and the Tuaregs were shouting and hitting. They were beating up the Susu. They hit him many times, and then they pulled him away, dragging him along, back inside. The screams continued from inside the walls as well. In the desert, you hear cries very clearly as they penetrate the night. I decided I would wait until everything was quiet.

Once the screams had gone silent, I got up and I walked ahead. I didn't know where I was going. Just ahead. Far. On the sand. Barefoot.

6

It was the middle of the night, and I was completely alone. I kept going, on foot. When you're in the desert, your feet sink into the sand, and it makes walking very tiring. The body feels as if it's taken on extra weight. Even so, I walked on, until four in the morning, through the immense darkness.

When I was too tired, I stopped and looked around me. The darkness was lifting, and that terrified me because I didn't know where I was. It was the desert, the empty desert, where only the snakes roam. A place where people die. But at that time, I didn't know all that. I lay down and went to sleep for six hours, until about ten in the morning.

I woke up and I looked ahead without knowing what ahead was. Whatever direction I looked in seemed the way ahead. And I couldn't see anything else. Always the desert. The desert here. The desert over there. The desert everywhere. Nothing else.

I continued on foot for another five hours until I felt a terrible need to drink some water. In Pulaar, when the body clamours for water, we call it *donka*. There's a word for it in French, but I've forgotten it. I felt a great *donka*, but it wasn't easy since there wasn't any water anywhere. *And now which way do I go?* I asked myself, and then I heard something. I heard the sound of a motor.

The sound was actually two hours away from me, but I heard it, and I heard it get nearer. In less than an hour, it came closer, and then more time passed. *Now I can hear it well*, I said to myself. *Yes, it's a motorbike. A motorbike on its own.*

It came towards me, and I started sweating. *If someone here sees me*, I thought, *they'll grab me and take me back to Taalanda.* Even so, I held out my hand and motioned for it to stop. What else could I do? I didn't know where I was, and the thirst was beginning to devour my whole body.

He stopped in front of me, thrusting his Kalashnikov behind him, and began to speak.

"Where are you going?" he asked in French.

"I'm going to Algeria, to Timiaouine," I answered.

"You'll never find your way from here to Timiaouine across the desert. You'll die before you get there."

"*Ah, bon?* Really?"

"Yes." He signalled for me to get on the back of his motorbike, and said he would take me part of the way. But I was afraid he might end up returning me to Taalanda.

"No, *merci*, I'll continue on foot," I said.

And again he said, "Climb on the bike, and I'll show you the way to Timiaouine."

I didn't trust him, because to me all the inhabitants of the desert seemed the same. But eventually I said, "*Oke*," and I climbed on the back of the motorbike.

In a short time, he turned off the motor and ordered me to get down. "Go that way, go, and you'll see." I didn't know what he was saying, what he wanted. He kept motioning me towards a place, and I approached it, trembling. And then I saw water. Yes, water. And a little further, there was a small gourd, made of goatskin. I don't know how many mouthfuls I drank. Ten, or twenty, but I felt I had a new body. Legs, stomach, arms, eyes—everything felt new. That's what water does. Water and your body.

I got back on the motorbike, and he brought me to a kind of fork. There, I got off the motorbike, and he raised the sleeves of his arms.

"Look, this way leads to Taalanda and that way to Timiaouine. When you go that way, in two hours you'll see a small tyre. Those tyres tell you you're on the right road.

"*Oke*," I said. "*Merci.*"

He gave me a packet of biscuits and a small *zipa* full of water.

"Keep following this path—you're fifty-five kilometres from Timiaouine."

"*Oke.*"

"In the desert, fifty-five kilometres is a lot—are you sure you can go on foot?" He waited for my answer.

"I have no other choice," I told him.

"If you give me a little money, I'll take you."

"I don't have any money."

"None at all?"

"No."

"*Oke,* then follow that path, but make sure you stay out of the way. They often have controls here, and it's better for you to remain hidden."

He started his motorbike and rode off in the direction of Taalanda.

7

I walked for nineteen hours until six the next morning. The mountains were sand, the valleys were sand, everything was sand. There, your steps immediately disappear and no one can say, "Yes, here, someone has come this way."

I'll continue for a little longer, I decided, and I continued walking for the whole day. I took off my trousers and wrapped them around my head so that the sun wouldn't beat down too hard on me. I went on for six hours, seven hours, I don't know. In the end, I thought, *I'm going to leave these here*, and I threw away my trousers because they felt too heavy. And I continued onwards. In my underpants, without shoes, on the burning sand. Taking smaller and smaller steps.

By nineteen zero zero hours, I had no water left, and I figured, *A man is going to die soon*. By *a man*, I meant this one here, me. Me and the desert. The endless desert.

But at times something appeared. *Yes, there's something over there*. At first, I thought it was a car, two cars, one here and another one over there. *It's the police*, I thought, panicking, but I had no choice and I kept going forward, in the direction of what I was seeing. In the end, I realised they weren't cars. They were *kifs*; there were two *kifs*, right there.

Kifs are giant plastic containers, and sometimes they're filled with water. At other times, they have petrol inside. They have a lid on top and a little water spout at the bottom. The Tuaregs leave them there, because they know that people are sometimes on foot and that it's not easy to walk in the desert. It's very hot, and thirst can overcome you. The Tuaregs know this, and that's why they leave these containers.

And there were two of them, two *kifs*. *I'll get closer*, I decided, and I walked towards them. *Voilà*, there, yes, there were two *kifs* and they were full, but I didn't know what was inside them, water or petrol. I started looking for the spout, and I saw two long inner tubes made of rubber, like those tubes you find inside bicycle tyres, attached to the tap. They had become tangled and they blocked the water spout. I didn't have enough strength in my fingers to untie them, so I tried with my teeth. With my top teeth and my bottom teeth, with all my teeth. Finally, I managed to free the knot, and the water started coming out, fast, from the *kif's* hole. Water was dripping down on me. Yes, water.

I opened my mouth and I drank. I drank a lot. Then, taking one of the tubesa, I tried to put some water into it. But the tube had holes in it, in four places. I took off my shirt, and with it I tied the tube to my body so that the holes weren't exposed. In that way, I would be able to have some water for the journey. *Now, I can go on*, I thought. And I went on.

Sometimes when you're in the desert, a powerful wind starts blowing. And then you can't even walk. You have to stop and protect yourself so that the sand can't hurt you. You might remain like that for a whole hour. Or two hours. Only when the wind has finally tired itself out, can you continue on your journey.

I continued on foot for three days. Seventy-two hours. Only ever drinking a little water. Always hiding along the way. Sometimes I was terrified. *There's someone over there*, I thought, and I stooped down. Then: *There's nothing there.* I kept on until I was too tired to keep going. Then I shut my eyes, and slept until I could open my eyes again. And then, once more, I walked ahead, until I was too tired to go on. In the end, I saw some lights in the distance. *That's Timiaouine over there*, I thought. And there it was.

Timiaouine, Algeria.

8

I arrived in Timiaouine at six in the morning. I saw a large mosque. *I must go and recite my prayers*, I thought, and I went in.

It's very important for me to recite my prayers, but I don't do it so that someone can see me and say, "Ibrahima is reciting his prayers, he's a good Muslim." No, it is all between God and me; it's our relationship.

When I finished praying, an old man approached me.

"*Salaam alaikum*," he said.

"*Alaikum salaam*," I answered him.

He realised I wasn't feeling well, and he offered me some bread—a little bit of bread and some juice. "*Shukran*," I said, and I swallowed everything. Later, I lay down on a bench and I went to sleep, fast asleep. My body. On the wood. Time passed. I slept for seven hours, and no one disturbed me.

When I woke up, my legs looked like they belonged to an elephant.

I couldn't walk with my legs like that, but I managed to leave the mosque and go into the street, I don't know how. I was sitting outside a small hostel when a boy walked by.

"You're Guinean," he said to me.

"Yes."

"You have very big legs."

"Yes."

He went into the hostel, and came back out with a cloth and some hot water. He started massaging my legs, down and up, down and up, one by one. Without saying a word.

When he had finished, he asked me a question: "*Ko honno wi'ete-dhaa*?" In our language, that means, "What's your name?"

"I am Ibrahima, and you?"

"I am Ismail."

9

Little Ismail is not like other people. Some people are very different from others, and Ismail is one of those. When I knew him, he was thirteen years old, and he was little, which is why I called him little Ismail. I don't know how old he would be now. Sixteen, maybe seventeen, I'm not sure. My father used to say that time did not pass in the same way for everyone, and that's true.

Ismail and I spent six months together. From our time in Timiaouine to our time in Ghardaïa. In Ghardaïa, we separated, and I didn't see him again after that. But now, when at any moment I feel my legs swelling up, I remember little Ismail.

One, because he gave me those massages. Down and up, down and up, one leg, then the other, for three days. Two, because I was then able to put on some shoes again and start to walk. Little by little, first one leg in front, then the other, and I could do this without pain. And three, because he showed me where to find work. Little Ismail did all of those things for me.

"In Timiaouine, there's a place where you can find work," he said to me one day. "We have to go to that place and stay on the side of the road, without moving, and wait for work."

"*Oke.*"

"Work will soon come our way, you'll see."

We went and waited a little—maybe a minute, two minutes—when an old man appeared in an ancient van. He took us to a place where there was a lot of rubble. "You have to load this into a wheelbarrow and then bring it here, to me," he told us.

He paid us two hundred dinars for each trip. To earn two hundred dinars took us about two hours, more or less; sometimes a little longer. Each day, we did this four times, so that every day he paid us eight hundred dinars, about six euros.

And that's what we did in Timiaouine for three weeks. Filling up the wheelbarrow with rubble and then emptying it. On the fourth week, we left for Bordj.

10

Coming from Mali, Bordj is the second city you encounter in Algeria. Sometimes they call it Bordj Mokhtar, but I like to shorten words. From Timiaouine to Bordj is one hundred and fifty-five *kilo*. When I say *"kilo,"* people here correct me and say kilometre. That's how it happens here, but in Africa, it's not like that, we prefer to shorten words. If you call it a kilometre, it makes the journey longer.

One hundred and fifty-five *kilo* to Bordj. But from Timiaouine to Bordj is not like going from Taalanda to Timiaouine. The sand is the same and so is the wind, but the road is paved, and that makes it easier—you can walk faster. One hundred and twenty *kilo* to Bordj. We were three: me, little Ismail, and a Malian. Sometimes we saw someone else, on the sand, a body, lying in a strange position. The face distorted by thirst, terrible thirst. That's what the desert is like. Ninety *kilo* to Bordj. The Malian couldn't take it anymore, and he stopped by the side of the road. We went on ahead. What else could we do? Sixty *kilo* to Bordj. Little Ismail spotted a very long snake crossing the road. We waited, half hidden, until the snake disappeared. In our country, if you do something to a snake, it will bring you bad luck, and so you give it priority and let it go its own way. Forty *kilo* to Bordj. We slept at night. We would lie down on the sand and sleep. Sleep is very important, to get back your strength and also to forget a bit. When you forget, your body feels lighter and it's easier to walk afterwards. Twenty-five *kilo* to Bordj. We spent four days and nights on the road, and on the fifth, we arrived in Bordj.

We spent two months working in Bordj, mixing cement. We slept next to the cement as well, and we woke up sweating. Work began at six in the morning and never finished. Some houses were reaching roof height, others were just starting from ground level, and there was a lot of cement to mix.

In the end, we started thinking about things. "The houses here are very big and we're very little," we figured. What I mean to say is that because we were little, we earned very little money. And so one day, I went to little Ismail.

"Why don't we go to another town?" I asked him.

"*Oke*," he answered.

We went to Reggane, hidden in the back of a pickup truck. There were sixteen people crammed into a space that was big enough to fit two goats, and we had to pay seventeen thousand dinar for the trip. "*Koto*, next time we'll take a bus," little Ismail said to me. And so we went from Reggane to Adrar by bus.

11

Adrar is a different world. There, there was no one at all who looked like us.

A woman went by. She was wearing a long cloak, a niqab. We asked her where we could find the bus for Ghardaïa, but she didn't answer. She walked straight ahead. We stayed where we were. A man came to us. He had a beard so long I ended up looking down at his feet. We asked him where the bus station was and he said: "It's over there, it's not far." On the way, we saw only beards and niqabs. And their stares told us: *This is not a place for you.*

When we reached the station, we waited in the queue to buy a ticket. When it was our turn, "*Salaam alaikum,*" I said to the woman behind the glass. And she answered: "A ticket to Ghardaïa costs one thousand one hundred dinars." I looked through my clothes, and I found one thousand and five hundred dinars. Little Ismail also tried, looking here and there until he'd searched his whole body, but he had nothing, zero dinars.

"You go ahead, Ibrahima," he said to me. "I'll stay here."

I looked to my right, to my left, I looked again, and I thought, *I can't leave this child here.*

We went out of the ticket office, and a taxi driver approached us. He studied our appearance and then he asked us if we were hungry. We answered that we were. He put his hand in his pocket and he took out a five hundred-dinar bill, but before putting it into our hands, he asked us this question: "Are you Muslims?" "Yes. Of course," we answered. He remained silent, looking at us for a long time. And then he handed us the bill.

"Now we have two thousand dinars," I said to Ismail, "and in order to buy two tickets to Ghardaïa, we only need two hundred more." And we remained sitting on the pavement, looking at the buses, considering our future.

In the end, some people who looked like us came by. They'd travelled from Cameroon, from the Ivory Coast, and from Mali. They told us that they wanted to go to the capital, to Algiers. We explained our situation to them, and they immediately started collecting money for us. Five dinars, ten, twenty, each gave what he could, until we reached two hundred.

"Now we have two thousand and two hundred dinars," little Ismail said to me, "and we can go to Ghardaïa."

And we went on to Ghardaïa.

12

I spent three months in Ghardaïa. Little Ismail stayed there for two months. Months mixing cement. Our boss wanted us to continue working for him, but little Ismail had different ideas.

"*Koto*," he said to me, "here we're making enough money, but we can make more in Algiers."

"No, Ismail," I answered, "I have to go on to Libya."

"Libya?" He was astonished. "Why Libya?" I hadn't told him anything until then.

I told him the story of my little brother. How he had left home and how I had followed him. "I know he's in Sabratha, because we spoke on the phone when I was still in Conakry, but since then, I haven't been able to talk to him again. I tried from Timiaouine, but no, impossible, impossible. Then I tried from Bordj, but from there as well, impossible. And finally, a lot of time has passed, and I've now spent five or six months without knowing where my little brother might have gone.

"And that's why, Ismail," I continued, "I have to go and look for Alhassane. Because he's a child, and our father is dead, and that means he is my responsibility. If I find him and I'm able to speak to him face to face, I know he will listen to me and return home."

"*Oke*," little Ismail agreed, "but once you've brought your brother back home, then what will you do?"

"I will live there, Ismail. I don't want to go to Europe. My destiny is in Guinea."

Ismail was silent. He looked down to the ground, as if confused. Little Ismail. In his face I always saw my own little brother, but I never told him that.

He raised his eyes from the ground and gave me a little hug.

"Good luck in Libya, *Koto*, may God help you."

"Goodbye, *miñan*, good luck to you too. And thank you so much for the hot water and for the way you rubbed my legs. *Jaarama buy*, Ismail."

That's how we said goodbye, and then I watched him walk along the road towards the station and slowly disappear.

13

Libya is a very different world. It is a place to make you suffer.

In Ghardaïa, people often warned me: "*Habibi*, don't go to Libya."

"I have no other choice," I answered them. "I have to go to Sabratha."

At that point, they explained the route to me: "First, you have to go to Debdeb by bus, and from there, you have to continue on foot. But be careful."

From Ghardaïa to Debdeb, one thousand and three hundred dinar. Seven hours.

Debdeb is Algeria's last town. After that is the border and after that, Libya. The border is an international zone. When you're there, you're not in Algeria and you're not in Libya—you're in the domain of the police. And the police aren't squeamish. They know what it is to torture someone.

And if that person is someone like me, they don't hit you on the legs or on the hands, they hit you between the legs or on the head. They know that in those places the pain lasts the longest.

At the Debdeb station, I saw eight people. They told me that they were going to try to cross the border that night and that, if I wanted to, I could join them. But I answered: "No, you go. I'll stay here." I knew that some people got it wrong, and I wanted to see what happened to them.

I stayed in the station, sitting on a bench, waiting for the morning. And then, the piercing brightness of the light, burning my eyes. But no sign of the eight people. Nor did they appear in the afternoon. *They succeeded*, I thought. *They got into Libya—I should have gone with them*. But I had said no, and here I was, sitting on a bench, waiting for the night to come.

In the afternoon, two Guineans arrived. They too wanted to go to Libya, and they asked me if I would like to join them.

"Yes," I answered.

"If you pay us, we'll help you," they said.

Those words surprised me. "Excuse me, but how will you help me? Do you have a pickup truck or what? If I am going on foot, I don't need to pay you anything."

"*Oke*," they agreed. "You're right." And the three of us waited there, until dark.

As we were waiting, I noticed that they talked a lot. In the end, my ears were getting tired and I thought, *These people aren't good company.* This is something you learn little by little, how to get to know someone by the words they let out.

Twenty-two hours zero zero.

"*Gorebe,* it's dark now, let's go," they said to me.

But I said: "No, I'm not going. I'm too afraid."

"*Ah, bon?*"

"Yes. But you go ahead." And they went. I waited a little until they were at a good distance. And then I followed them.

I walked for three or four hours, on the sand, keeping the two Guineans in my sight.

At four in the morning, I realised that we were in Libya. We had arrived in a small village called Ghadames, and I began to see that things were not the same as in Algeria. *Allahu Akbar.* An old man was the first to go into the mosque to pray. He was carrying a large gun over his shoulders. *Allahu Akbar.*

This is Libya, I thought.

14

Allahu Akbar, the call to prayer, was being chanted from the minarets. An Arab came towards me and asked me what I was doing in front of the mosque.

"I've just come from prayer," I said, "and now I would like to go to work." I was wearing dirty trousers, like a labourer's.

"*Oke.*"

He believed me and then he explained: "There's no work here. You have to go to Tripoli, or to Sirte. There's a lot of work there."

"And how can I get there?"

"*Sir, yallah.*" Those words in Arabic mean "Let's go." Meaning, I was to follow him.

We crossed a few streets, and he brought me to a garage, a large and very wide garage. It was full of pick-ups.

"I want to go to Sabratha," I explained to him.

"You'll have to give me the money here," he said to me. "One hundred and fifty Libyan dinars."

They use dinars in Libya, as they do in Algeria. It's the same name, but it's not the same value. In general, it's very hard to understand how money works. A Libyan dinar has the same value as a European euro, so that one hundred and fifty Libyan dinars is a hundred and fifty euros. This is what they told me.

"One hundred and fifty dinars?" I asked.

"Exactly," he answered.

That's a lot money, I thought, and I asked him to wait.

"That's fine. Go and take a walk along the streets. I'll be here."

I walked along the streets of Ghadames, wondering what to do, worried. I couldn't find any other transport to

Sabratha. I returned to the first garage and went up to the Arab. He was cleaning a pickup truck, a Nissan. He didn't turn his head. "One hundred and fifty dinars," I said to him again. I put the money into his hands, and he wrote my name on a list.

15

When the pickup was ready, they lined us up as if we were merchandise, and they threw a heavy cover over us. The whole cover smelt of something, maybe burnt meat. We couldn't see anything from under the cover, and I became a little angry. Words came out of me, I don't know from where.

"I can't travel anywhere if I can't see where I'm going," I said.

The driver took his Kalashnikov, and opened the skin of my head with the butt of his gun. I still have the scar here—can you see it? And then he started shouting: "If you don't think you're going to Sabratha, why did you get onto this pickup?"

"*Oke*," I bowed to him. "I'm sorry." Everyone became silent. That's how they subjugate you. There is nothing you can say.

I don't know how many hours we were on the road, under that cover. If you can't see any light, it's hard to measure time accurately. It was always night under there, night and the smell of burnt meat. I could only sense time by feeling the changes on my head, as the blood began to dry.

At some point, the pickup came to a stop, somewhere in the darkness, in the vastness of the desert. And they ordered all of us to get out. We were twelve or thirteen *kilos* from Sabratha.

"From here, you go straight ahead on foot," they told us. "But *yallah, yallah*, come on, walk fast, you have to get there before sunrise." The law in that place is that if the police catch you, they return you to Debdeb, or they send you to prison.

"*Habibi*, hurry, *yallah, yallah*." The driver was showing us the way with his gun. "Four, five, six," he yelled, showing us his watch. "Faster, *yallah*, get a move on." We quickly started on our way. It was unbelievably hot and we were thirsty, but there wasn't any water and there wasn't any time. It was four in the morning, and *yallah, yallah*.

Six people arrived in Sabratha. I was among them. The others remained behind, in the middle of the desert. Maybe they were taken by the police. Or thirst. I don't know.

16

When I arrived in Sabratha, someone who looked like one of my kind approached me. He told me that if I was looking for a European *program*, I was to follow him.

"I know the place from where they all take off," he said.

"Baba Hassan?" I asked.

And he nodded yes with his head. "That's where we're going."

The Baba Hassan camp, or *trankilo,* is huge and wide open. There, if you want to find a place to lie down, there's the sand on the ground. If you look up, you see that there's no roof over you, everything is open to the sky. If you look to the left, you see only migrants. It's the same to the right. We were over six hundred in that camp, many from Guinea.

Before I could go to sleep, they asked for my name. "Balde, Ibrahima." And my age. "Seventeen." A man with a long beard was making notes, and he had some doubts. He asked me again, "What year were you born?"

"The fourth of August 1999," I replied, "in Conakry."

"*Oke,*" he said to me, and he wrote that down. Since that day, I've been officially five years younger than my real age.

They had taught me that trick in Algeria: "When you go to Libya, it's important for you to say you're younger than eighteen years old. That way, they can't put you in prison, and if you don't go to prison you have a chance of surviving." And so, in front of that man with the long beard, I was born for a second time, but in 1999. But I hadn't changed the day: 8/4: the fourth of August.

After that, they took down some other dates, but I was half asleep and I don't remember much. I do remember what they said to me: "From now on, you're a Baba Hassan person. And in order to get onto the European *program*, you can't go to any other group. Your price will be decided by Baba Hassan, and once you've paid, we'll tell you when you can go."

"*Oke*," I answered. I hadn't explained to them why I had come to Libya, because I was afraid they would throw me out, or take a stick and break one of my bones.

That's how things work in Sabratha. They stock up the migrants in some area in order to organise their traffic. And once they've got you in a particular camp, you're not allowed to embark with any other group.

The other day, someone from here told me that Europeans give a lot of money to block the Libyan migrant trade, and that's why there are a lot of people like me in Libyan prisons. I don't know if that's true, I don't understand politics that well, but I know very well what kind of a place Libya is.

Libya is one vast prison, and it's very difficult to get out of there alive.

17

It was six in the morning, and as soon as I lay down, I fell asleep. Maybe two, maybe three hours, no more. Suddenly, I woke up. "Alhassane? *Miñan?*" I had to find his trail. I moved around the *trankilo*, looking from person to person. But no, "Alhassane is not here." I despaired and I went out into the street.

Taf-taf. A street in Sabratha is not like a street in Conakry. In Sabratha, there's no one about. Only some fallen houses. Occasionally a pickup truck, going very fast. Some shots. *Taf-taf.* And that's it. Silence. That's what Libya is like. It's not a place for anyone to be alive.

I had brought a small photograph with me, and whenever I could, I showed it to the people in the camp and asked. "*Miñan*, yes, my little brother, Alhassane. Have you seen him?" Some took the picture in their hands, they looked carefully, and then they said, "No, I haven't seen him."

Others said, "Yes."

"Yes?"

"Yes, I recognise him, but it's a long time since I've seen him—he's not around here anymore." Some others didn't even stop; they didn't have the time.

A child told me that Baba Hassan had other camps. "Baba Hassan is one person, but he has a lot of houses in Libya. Two in Sabratha, two in Zawiya, and more in Tripoli.

"*Ah, bon?*"

"Yes, Baba Hassan is very rich. He earns a lot of money from the migrants. And as soon as he earns more money, he buys more houses."

"*Ah, bon?*"

18

I spent two days in Sabratha. And there, two days feel very long, even longer than two days in the desert without water. Because you can't get anywhere. You walk. You stop. You look. You walk to the next street. You run. You hide. You look again. You don't see anything moving. You come out of hiding. You go on. Stop. Another street corner. You scan. No one. The Arabs are all invisible, but you know they're there. You hear gunshots, but you don't know where they're coming from.

Then the night comes down. It gets darker, but not quieter. From time to time, you hear more gunshots. And you begin to shiver. Now you're really trembling. You're in the street. You're not sure where you're going. Stop. You see the village. The village is still. Another gunshot. You keep going. You stop. You're here. Looking at the village. Watching. Watching out for the one who is looking for you. To keep them from finding you, you have to keep walking. Until you fall asleep. Wherever you are.

Another two shots. *Taf-taf.* You dive down. You get up again. You keep going. You don't know where to. *I'll go back to the* trankilo. You see the village. Everything is still. *Why did I come here?* you ask yourself. And you call out for Alhassane, in a low voice. You call out twice. Another gunshot. *Taf.* To keep you quiet. "Yes, sorry." You're terrified. Your own voice terrifies you. Your footsteps terrify you.

"Alhassane Alhassane Alhassane. Where are you?"

You have to keep moving. You go on. You don't know where you're going. You stop. You fall down. You stay down.

The day is breaking. You open one eye. You're still alive.

Sabratha is a puzzle. This piece goes here. That piece goes over there. But you can't get from one piece to the other. There are controls everywhere. They hold the power, those men who have the guns. Very often, they're no more than children, little boys with a grenade in their hand and a Kalashnikov slung over their shoulders. One day, one of them made me stop and he said to me: "You all, you Africans, we're going to stick this up your arse and, *taf-taf-taf*, we'll kill you all."

19

There was no trace of Alhassane in Sabratha. *I'm going to go to Zawiya*, I decided. From Sabratha to Zawiya is close, no more than one night on foot. I don't know how long it takes by day, because you can't walk by day. The police will catch you and throw you into prison or break your bones, simply because you are who you are.

I waited until night. *Zawiya*, I thought. The sun went down.

I walked on foot, on the side of the road. I did it in threes: I looked. I moved. I stopped. I did this again. Look. Move. Stop. And again.

It was five in the morning. No one was about. Everything was quiet. It was six in the morning, and I was beginning to feel tired. I saw a mosque on the side of the road, and next to it, a tree. Don't ask me where that was. It was night, there was a tree, that's all I know. *I'll hide and rest here*, I thought. I bent down and checked all around the tree. *There's no one here, I can close my eyes for a bit.* Three seconds. *I had better open my eyes, just in case.* No one. I closed my eyes again and fell asleep. Until nine in the morning.

When I woke up, the tree was still there, next to the mosque. Nothing was moving, anywhere, and I was terrified. In Libya, it's not a good sign if a lot of time passes and you can't see anything moving. *I have to get out of here*, I thought. *Yes, I've spent much too much time here.*

It was ten or eleven in the morning, and I was walking in the sun. It was hot, scorching hot. Suddenly, a pickup truck went by, and I bent down and hid. *It's gone*, Allahu Akbar. I walked on. But then I heard steps, coming behind me. Yes, footsteps. I turned my head and I saw an old man coming my way. I took quicker steps. Even quicker now. In vain. Two hands on my back. Two hands and something else. *He's caught me.*

He started in Arabic: "*Barka lafi.*"

I don't speak Arabic very well, so after greeting him, I answered: "Excuse me, I don't understand what you're saying."

And then he asked me something: "*Barka lafok?*"

"No," I answered.

"No?" he asked.

"No."

And then he lifted his *guba* and showed me his Kalashnikov. The *guba* is a kind of long jacket, which the men wear. And you know what a Kalashnikov is.

I climbed into his four-wheel drive. I don't know if it was a Golf or a Ford, I can't remember now, but it was a large car. In the front were guns. I sat in the back. He spoke to me in Arabic, and I couldn't understand a thing he said.

20

I was put against a wall for twenty-four hours, my head bowed, with someone standing behind me the whole time. He told me to call my village and ask someone for money.

"I don't have anyone I can call in my village," I explained to him, in vain. "I don't have a father. My mother is poor, she works her small garden, and there's no one to look after me." I tried to make him understand all this in Arabic, but it was always useless.

The area was surrounded by a large wall. It was completely open to the sky.

At twelve noon, the sun was high up in the sky and beat down on the sand. The man behind me ordered me to go down on my knees.

"Stay on your knees and raise your arms." And he left me there, with my arms raised and a heavy rock in each hand. "If you drop your arms, I'll shoot you."

"*Oke.*"

And the worst time began.

Time weighed heavy on me, and the rocks began to shake. The rocks first, and then my arms and then my chest and then my neck and then my head and then everything. Shaking. And if you fall to the ground, the sand burns you even more. The sun feels like burning water in your mouth. And now, the man takes his gun and hits you where it hurts the most, *paf, paf, paf.* But for him, it's nothing. For him, it's a small matter, a bit of bother. For a man like that, torture is like saying "Hello." And if he doesn't kill you, you had better say, "Thank you."

After a while, he brought me half a cup of water. Thirst had knotted up my whole body, and I drank a little. But he quickly took the cup away from my lips. I asked for more water, and I got a punch instead. To stop the thirst. "You've drunk enough." A half cup of water.

Yes, enough water not to die. That was his plan: for me to suffer but not to die. Once I was dead, I wouldn't be worth anything, and I wouldn't be able to call anyone and beg them to send me money. That's why, occasionally, he gave me half a cup of water.

Two half-cups of water. Three days.

I spent three whole days there, and someone tortured me twenty-four hours a day. But I wasn't the only one. There were another hundred people with me, or maybe even more than a hundred—I don't know, I didn't count them. But I could hear them, men and women. I didn't hear any children. The women were crying, and screaming through the whole night. They never stopped. One would go quiet, and then another would start, and when she went quiet yet another one started up. And so on, *next*.

Our torturers were all civilians, people like you and me. The tortured were also all the same, men and women. They all looked like me. No one had done anything to deserve this. I had wanted to go and look for my little brother in Libya; others had dreamed of going to Europe. But they tortured us all the same.

I didn't want to talk about all of these things because, as I describe them, I see them all again, in front of my eyes, at the same time as I'm explaining everything. You are right here, now, listening to me, but I'm back there, it's all taking place again in my head, and as I'm telling you about it, I'm living all of it all over again. That's why I didn't want to talk about all of this. But you asked me, and I've told you. And as I'm describing all of these things, I'm feeling them all over again.

21

In the end, the old man who had brought me to the torture place understood something: *No one is going to send any money to get this boy out.* And so, he took me out of that place and made me get into his four-wheel drive again. He took me to a place I didn't know. It was a dark street corner.

Another old man arrived, a different old man, a new one. The two old men started talking in front of me, but I couldn't understand anything. Arabic is a very difficult language anyway, and the two old men were speaking very fast.

The new old man looked at me for a long time: he studied my whole body, from top to bottom and from bottom to top. Again and again. He didn't ask me anything; he only looked. And I was terrified because they were both carrying guns. I didn't know if they were planning to kill me. I didn't know what other plans they might have for me. And the new old man kept looking me over, again and again.

In the end, he stopped looking at me and began to take out some bills. One by one, he counted the bills and gave them to the other old man. In all, he gave him three hundred Libyan dinars. I counted them with my own eyes. Three hundred in all. And I understood: *This street corner is a market, and three hundred dinars is my price.* Yes, they were selling and buying me as they would a goat.

The first old man put all the bills into his *guba*, started up his car, and drove off. Just like that. He didn't even say goodbye to me.

22

I don't know how old the man I'm now talking about was. He could have been sixty or maybe seventy years old, but I can't tell you precisely because I can't distinguish age very well. In Guinea, it would be very hard to meet an old man like that. But I can tell you that the man who sold me was old, and that the man who bought me was even older. His beard was much longer as well.

He also had a four-wheel drive, like the other old man. I sat in the back. I can't remember what we spoke about. The old man could speak a little bit of French, but I didn't feel like talking. It was night-time, and the world was very dark. I didn't know where we were going. Perhaps if I had asked him he would have told me, but I didn't ask him anything.

I remember that we stopped in front of a large iron door. We went in and found ourselves in a large building. The walls were made of metal—it was a kind of hangar. And this hangar was full of chickens. And chickens are never quiet. The old man went towards a feeding trough, and the chickens all followed him, hundreds of chickens. All crazy. He threw some food on the ground, and all the hundreds of chickens started to peck at it.

After that, the old man came to me.

"Did you see all that?" he asked.

"Yes," I answered.

"This is now your work. You give the grain to the chickens, twice a day, every day." It was some kind of small grain, what do you call it? Corn. Yes. That's what it was. "After that, you look for the eggs and you put them in a cardboard box, in this *albiol*," he ordered.

"*Oke*," I answered.

He told me he would return every night to pick up the *albiol* and to bring me something to eat. "Otherwise, you'll just have to eat the corn. *Oke?*"

"*Oke.*"

"Until tomorrow then," he said.

"Until tomorrow." And he left me there, in that large hangar, with the hundreds of chickens. Eating with the chickens, sleeping with the chickens, everything with the chickens. Yes, that's what I did.

In the morning, I woke up very early because it wasn't easy to get any sleep in that hangar. The chickens would start to screech, and I would be thinking of Alhassane. And then, I got up, mixed the corn, spread it out on the ground with a bowl, and called out to the chickens, "*Kotz-kotz-kotz.*"

Afterwards I started to look for the eggs. Sometimes I filled thirty-five *albiol*, sometimes forty. When it was dark, the old man returned and gave me biscuits, bread, and some juice to drink. "*Merci,*" I said to him. We would speak for a short time, and then he would leave. He always locked the door two times, *klak-klak.*

The next day, the same. *Kotz-kotz-kotz*, look for eggs, fill the *albiol,* lie down, get up, *kotz-kotz-kotz* . . . But I had a plan: *I'll do everything this old man tells me to do, and then maybe his spirit will be moved and he'll begin to change. He'll realise I am a human being as well. And then, he'll help me.* But very often, you believe something and it turns out not to be true.

23

I was in that place for nine days. Me and the chickens, the hundreds of chickens. All crazy. Sometimes I spent the whole day without eating. The old man would come halfway through the night and give me a bit of bread, *kotz-kotz-kotz.* He asked me if any of the chickens had died and I said, "No. *Tout est en ordre.* Everything is in order."

"*Oke.*" And he would leave again. And always before driving off, he locked the door, twice, *klak-klak.*

On the tenth day, the old man turned up as it was getting dark. He gave me some biscuits and a little water to drink, and started to count the *albiol*: "One, two, three, four . . ." I don't know what number he got to, but his phone began to ring. I remember how flustered the chickens were. The old man started shouting, "*Allo? Allo? Allo?*" He said *"Alo"* three times and then he ran out. He started his motorbike, and in a flash he was gone.

He'd forgotten to close the door. No *klaks*: he hadn't locked it. I noticed that immediately, but still I waited. Twenty minutes, thirty minutes, forty minutes—I don't know how long. I waited until I could feel confident. In the end, I saw that the old man hadn't returned, and I escaped, running.

I noticed some trees, a small wood, and behind it there was a sandy hill. From there, you could see all around, and in the distance, the lights of a town. *Zawiya*, I thought. *I'll go down there and find the* trankilo *of Baba Hassan*. I began to run, as fast as I could, *yallah, yallah*.

When I entered the *trankilo* for the first time, I kept looking back, checking everything with my eyes. And I thought to myself, *I've escaped from the old man, but not from my terror.*

And since that night, that's how I've lived, with this terror that someday I'll see the old man again. Because I know that if I ever run into him, he'll eliminate me. *Taf.* That's it. It won't trouble him in the least. And that terror now lives in my body. Sometimes, even when I'm asleep, I remember. I see the old man, the old man and his chickens, hundreds of chickens. All crazy. And him as well.

24

I stayed two days in Zawiya, asking everyone in the camp. I kept showing the small photograph I had.

"Yes, *miñan*, Alhassane? No?"

"No."

Again and again, in vain. There was no trace of my little brother there either, and I went back to Sabratha, walking at night.

Two Guineans helped me. We took a route through the mountains so as not to run into the old man. *Yes, otherwise, he'll simply eliminate me*, I thought. *He won't think twice about doing it.*

When I got back to Sabratha, I searched again through all the camps. The two that belonged to Baba Hassan and another seven. In those as well, there was a lot of stock. All migrants, all waiting for their chance. But I didn't find Alhassane. "Go to Sirte," they told me, "he's probably there, or if not there, in Tripoli. Go there and have a look." But I didn't go; I didn't have enough money. My companions gave me something to eat as well: they held out their hands and put a little couscous into mine.

I spent two months in Sabratha. Two months. Two months searching. Until I was worn down. I became so worn out, I lost the fear of death. One night, I woke up and I thought, *The life I'm leading here has no meaning. I would prefer death. Or else I need to find* miñan, *Alhassane. But if I can't find him, I would like to die.*

25

It was Friday.

I had slept in Baba Hassan's *trankilo*, and I had gone from there to the mosque. Friday prayers are very important for us. You can skip other prayers, but never Friday prayers. And so, I'd gone to the mosque to pray. I was making my way back to the *trankilo*, along the backstreets of Sabratha. Walking with me was a Guinean friend, a Fula, called Dimedi.

"Ibrahima," he suddenly said to me.

"Yes?"

"You're suffering a lot here, and everyone is keeping things from you, but today I want to talk to you about something."

I stopped walking for a moment. "What is it?" I asked him.

"Shall we keep walking?" he asked.

"No. Who is hiding something from me here? If you happen to know something, tell me, I beg you."

"Yes, I want to say something to you, but you must listen very carefully to me. If I can show courage in this way, then you too must also show courage."

I looked him straight in the eyes and said, "*Oke*, you can start."

And he started.

"You've come here looking for your little brother, isn't that so?"

"Yes."

"I know your little brother. We were often together, we both slept next to each other, with him there and me here, under the same cover. I didn't know that he had an older brother, because he never said anything about that. But, yes, now I realise you're his brother and I can see how much you've suffered since coming to Libya. All for the sake of that child."

As he was speaking, I remained silent. I heard his words, I listened, and I thought: *One, Alhassane is in prison. Two, I'll go and look for him, it doesn't matter where. Three, I'll get him out of prison and we'll go home, to Guinea.*

"Do you know where he is?" I asked.

"No," he answered, "I don't know where he is, but I do know that at some point, there was a *naufrage*."

He had told me everything in Pulaar, but he used that one French word. Just one word: *naufrage*. It was the first time I heard that word.

"I don't understand what you're saying. What is it you want to tell me?"

85

"It's not easy," he answered. "When there is an accident with one of the inflatable boats, that's what we call it, a *naufrage*."

"*Naufrage?*"

"Yes, a *naufrage*."

I thought a little, and I asked him, "So you're telling me that Alhassane ended up getting on a boat."

"Yes, you've understood what I've been trying to tell you, but that's not all. Alhassane didn't go by himself. There were one hundred and forty-four people on that boat."

Naufrage. Shipwreck. It was the first time I had contemplated that word. "One hundred and forty-four people." It had never occurred to me that so many people could fit on one of those small inflatable boats they call Zodiacs. I had learned two new things that morning, and I felt that it was more than enough.

"*Oke*," I said, "shall we go back to the *trankilo?*" And we went back to the Baba Hassan camp.

I lay down on some scattered cardboard and I closed my eyes, sunk in thought. I didn't understand. Miñan, *why did you want to go to Europe? We hadn't discussed this and agreed to it together. I told you you had to continue school. I told you your eyes were too big.*

Yes, big eyes and fourteen years old when I last saw him. He was a child.

I started beating my head against the cardboard on the ground, and my spirit left me. Once your spirit starts to

86

leave you, it's very hard to hold on. *First I lost my father in Conakry. Now I've lost my little brother in Libya. How can I explain all this to my mother?*

In the end, my spirit came back to me, little by little, and settled back in its place. I thought one hundred and forty-four people on an inflatable boat was too many. *No, it's not possible.*

I went to a friend of mine and I asked him: "Brother, in your opinion, is it possible to get one hundred and forty-four people on a Zodiac?"

"Ibrahima," he answered, "a hundred and forty-four people is nothing. In Libya, you can even see one hundred and eighty people on one of those Zodiacs. It's completely normal."

"*Oke,*" I said to him. And I took the photograph out of my pocket. "Now tell me the truth. You've been here for many months, in Sabratha. Did you know this child?"

He spent a long time looking, first at the picture and then at me. He thought for a long time. "No," he said at last, "I didn't know him."

26

I left the Baba Hassan camp and walked along the streets. There was no one about. A gunshot. Taf. I didn't have any intention of living any longer. A pickup went by. Four gunshots. Taf-taf-taf-taf. I was without fear. *You can shoot, I won't complain, I'll actually thank you.* You see, I loved that child so much. He was the sole purpose of my life—to catch him when he fell, to protect him when he needed it, and to help him learn at school. He was a lively child, and he was a boy. Father had said this to me, and Mother as well. Everyone had said, "He's a boy, thank God." Yes, but now there had been a *naufrage*. With one hundred and forty-three people on board and Alhassane, the hundred and forty-fourth.

But that, in Libya, is nothing.

Part III

Part III

I

In Libya, there is a lot of stock, the *trankilos* are full, and the prisons are also full.

Taf-taf-taf: "One of these days, we'll kill you all." It was a child who said this to me as he looked straight into my eyes. I think I told you this before, but it doesn't matter, I'm telling you this again so that you won't forget, so that you'll know what Libya is. The Arabs from there are good-looking, they have light skin, but they have a dark cavern inside them. And a Kalashnikov. The Kalashnikov has now become their body. It's the same for boys and girls, old people or children: the only thing these people can think of is *taf-taf-taf.*

The sea is also helping them. But the sea doesn't begin with the seashore. The sea starts in the *trankilo.* Each *campo* is filled with its own immigrant stock, and organises its own *program.* You give them the money, three thousand, or three thousand five hundred, and sometimes even more. Baba Hassan often wants more. And then they put you on a list, and when that list is full they organise an inflatable boat, a Zodiac.

If the Zodiac doesn't arrive in Europe, it's all the same to Baba Hassan. Baba Hassan still gets his money. If, before embarking, a soldier on the shore stops you, it's all the same. Baba Hassan still gets his money. Or if, when you get to the boat, you're suddenly frightened and you don't dare get on, it's all the same. Baba Hassan takes out his Kalashnikov and, *taf*, he kills you. Yes, one shot is enough. That's how it goes.

I'll explain all this to you.

Everything to do with the Zodiac takes place at night. It's inflated on the shore, and everything happens at the very last moment. Until then, you're there, waiting, in some corner. Once they've finished inflating the boat, the Libyans start shouting: *"Yallah, yallah,* faster, faster," It's time to leave. Sometimes you're wearing a short *guba*, a kind of life vest. More often than not, there are one hundred *gubas*, but the *program* has sent one hundred and fifty people. That means fifty people will get on with nothing at all. But at that moment, everything is *yallah, yallah,* and you'd better not ask any questions.

The Libyans begin to push the Zodiac out to sea, and they start the motor. This movement feels very strange to you because you have never before been on the water. Probably, you've never even looked at the sea with your own eyes before, but this is not the moment to ask questions. Here you are, sitting on top of the water, and it's time to go.

Here is Libya, there is Tunisia, and over there, Italy. And in between these places, there is only the sea. And the sea is a lottery. You know that a lot of people don't make it to the other shore, but the Libyans are shouting at you. "*Yallah, yallah,*" they keep repeating. The sea may be rough, but it's all the same, they continue to shove you into the Zodiac, they're not worried about what problems might lie ahead. The only thing they want to do is fill the Zodiac, and the fuller it is, the better for them.

Some people, terrified, suddenly say no, they don't want to get on, and in the end, they stay there without getting on the boat. The Arabs scream at them: "Those who want to go, get on, *yallah*, faster." And the ones who are too frightened remain on the beach, still wearing their *gubas*.

That one falls down first, taf. One shot is enough. If they die on the shore, they can't ask for their money back. Nor can they return to the *trankilo* and tell the others what they've seen in the port. Because that would frighten people, and this could reduce Baba Hassan's clientele. And that would not be good for Baba Hassan. And so the Libyans never force anyone to get on the boat, but they kill the ones who refuse to get on, right there, in front of everyone else's eyes. Taf.

Sometimes I think: *Will I ever find a way to forget all that?* It's as if my head were a cupboard. Now, in order to take something out of the cupboard, you have to have something else to put in there. In that way, new things make you get rid of old things. But for me, here, while I'm asking for asylum, I have nothing to do. I don't have work, I don't have friends, and so I don't have anything new to put into the cupboard.

All of my memories stay there, in that cupboard, fixed. And every day, they attack me.

2

We were two boys in our family. Not three. Two. Now I'm alone. I have two little sisters and my mother. But I can't ask my mother to help me. A man can do things a woman is not capable of doing. That's what they taught me. And I have to confess something to you: in Africa, losing a brother is not the same as losing a sister. I'm not talking about sadness, but about worry. When I say worry, what I want to say is responsibility, the responsibility of having to carry your family on your back. I know this well: if Alhassane at this moment is drowned in the sea, it means that I remain alone to battle things out. I'm condemned to do this, like so many others of my kind.

But the place where I should be battling isn't here. My destiny is not here. Not in Libya, not in Europe. I wanted to live the life of a truck driver: from Conakry to Nzérékoré, and from Nzérékoré to Conakry, and by doing this work, to help my family. But Alhassane escaped from home, and I had to go in search of him.

If I had found him, I would have sat next to him and I would have talked to him. For a long time. I would have explained things to him once more, how it has been from the moment we were born until now, and how we could plan our future together. Until he heeded my words. That's because I am the older of the two.

But I wouldn't have hit him, the way my father might have wanted me to. Or my mother. I could not, ever, hit my younger brother the way Father often hit me. I never knew how to behave like my father, and often my mother would get angry with me. "Now your arm is your father's arm," she would say to me. "If he doesn't do something well, you have to hit him, so that he'll learn." "Yes, Mother," I would say. I would give into her but, when the time came, I could never do it. One, because my father had a long belt, but I didn't have one. Two, because I never had the strength to hit hard. And three, because I'm not my father. And so I sat next to Alhassane and I spoke to him, the way I am speaking to you now.

And if I had been able to find him, I would have spoken to him one more time, in just this way. I wouldn't have done anything else. Speaking. Speaking to him with my eyes as well. In that way, the words wouldn't fall onto the ground.

3

For three days, I didn't drink anything, I didn't eat anything. I couldn't. My friends offered me things, but I said, "No." Whether it was my body or my mind doing this, I don't know. I'd lost my balance. I couldn't see my way. I sat on the ground and I thought, *Where am I?* I wasn't there. I asked myself: *Who am I speaking with right now?* I wasn't speaking with anyone. People were strangers. And I was a stranger. Legs. Hands. The body. All strangers.

Jaarama buy. That means "Thank you" in our language. Did I tell you that already? Forgive me, I'm going mad. When someone offered me something, I said, "*Jaarama buy*." And if they didn't offer me anything, I said the same thing, "*Jaarama buy*." Words of a stranger. And I, a stranger. All strangers. I was like that for three days.

On the fourth day, I went out to look for Alhassane.

"*Naufrage,* shipwreck," they had said to me. But I wasn't sure anymore, and I kept looking for him. In the same place, among the same people. I would approach someone and show them the photograph. "Yes, that's *miñan,* my little brother, have you seen him?" And then I asked: "Do you think it's possible to have one hundred and forty-four people on one Zodiac?" Some said to me that, no, it wasn't possible.

Part III

A whole week. Ten days. Two weeks. Three. There. A mere mouthful for the sea.

I was becoming a completely different person.

I went out into the street. *I don't see the purpose of continuing with this life*, I said to myself. *I prefer to die.* I looked at the life ahead of me, and I felt nothing but exhaustion. I was going mad. Yes, a madman walking through the deserted streets of Sabratha. I heard gunshots, and I didn't even pay any attention to where they could be coming from. Now into another street. Look. Stop. The Kalashnikovs didn't frighten me anymore. The desire for death eats up all fear.

But not completely. For example, I had no desire to be found by the old man with the chickens and have him kill me on the spot. *Taf.* In Libya, death is a banal event. And I didn't want to give the old man that pleasure. But I did want to die. Or not. I don't know.

I didn't know what I wanted. It's hard to explain this to you, because you haven't lived through that sort of thing, you haven't known Libya. But I had turned into someone different, I couldn't find any resemblance to what I was before. If an Arab had said something to me, I would have told him what I was thinking and added: "Now you decide what you want to do with me, and if you want, you can kill me." But in any case they didn't kill me, not even when I showed them the picture of my little brother:

"No?"

"No."

"*Oke.*"

And I went on looking for him.

4

Emi is from Cameroon. I met him in Sabratha, in Baba Hassan's *trankilo*. I don't know where he is now; I don't even know if he is alive. Possibly yes, *inshallah*. He lifted me out of those dark and filthy Libyan waters.

"Ibrahima, you are fighting with ghosts," he said to me.

Emi had a different way of communicating, and sometimes it was hard to follow him.

"Ibrahima, you'll never be able to find what you're looking for," he explained to me, "or it may be that now, you are actually looking for something else."

"I don't understand you, Emi," I answered.

"You're looking for some kind of punishment," he said. You need someone to beat you, or take you prisoner and torture you."

"*Ah, bon?* Really?"

"Yes. You're carrying a heavy load of guilt, and you need someone to punish you until you die. And so, if you yourself agree with that, then all right, be done with it." And he was silent. For three seconds, or maybe four, and then he went on: "You have to try to live, Ibrahima. You have to get that dirty sea out from inside you and start to walk on this earth and feel fear and pain, like the rest of us."

"You don't know what my pain is, Emi," I answered, "You haven't lost your little brother the way Ibrahima has."

"That's so," he agreed. "You're right, and for Emi, words are hard to come by just now. And so, I am going to mention something else to you: would you like to come and work with me tomorrow morning?"

He told me that he knew of a small building site next to Sabratha, in Zintan. The bosses were Arabs, but they were not like the ones I knew. He would explain to them that I was his friend, and he believed they would probably give me work.

"I have to think about it, Emi," I told him.

He waited.

"Did you think about it?"

"Yes, I did. I am not going to that building site. Emi, I know where I escaped from, and I'm afraid of seeing people like that again."

"Ibrahima, you don't need to be afraid of anyone there. No one knows you, you can work and they'll pay you."

"Can you guarantee it will be like that?"

"Yes."

"*Oke*." I gave in.

The next morning, I went to the building site with Emi. We spent the whole day there moving bricks. Picking up bricks and laying down bricks. That was my work. That and Alhassane. When I say Alhassane, I mean he was my guilt—I had failed my responsibility, I had been guilty of negligence.

One evening, I went to Emi and I said to him, "Emi, I'm tired of being here. I want to return to Algeria. Can you help me find some transport?"

"*Oke*," he answered.

5

I returned to Algeria in a pickup truck, just me, by myself with the driver, who was an Arab. The driver told me to come and sit in the front, and that's what I did. The windows of the truck cabin were tinted. That way, people can't see you from the outside in, but you can see them. You could see everything from the windows of that Land Cruiser.

Except that the everything you can see is actually nothing. Nothing at all. The empty desert. Sand, and then more sand. If, today, the two of us were there and you said to me, "Help me get to Algeria," I would never be able to find the way. I could look at the desert, but I wouldn't know which way to go. But the Arabs do; the Arabs know the desert well.

Before the Land Cruiser reached the border, we stopped in a small village.

"Get down here," the driver ordered me.

I did what he asked.

"Libya stops right here," he explained, "and from here you have to go by foot."

"*Oke.*"

This was not a problem for me, as I had walked that way before when I had first come into Libya, that night I was following the two Guineans. I knew how to cross that border. And so, in the afternoon at seventeen zero zero, I took some water from the fountain in Ghadames and continued on foot.

I moved through the night, walking on the sand, and as the light began to break, I approached Algeria. The village of Debdeb, which borders Libya, is where Algeria begins.

At the Debdeb station, in a corner, there is a small fountain. *I'm going to pray*, I decided, and I went to the fountain. Before you pray, you have to wash your face. Three times. And then your hands, also three times, slowly, very slowly, all the way up to the elbows. Then comes the head. And the hair. You're only supposed to wet your hair, but the water has to spread and penetrate to the head. And last, the feet. The feet need to be washed three times as well. *Voilà*. And now you can pray.

That's what I did, and I gave thanks to God that Libya was now over.

6

More than half of Algeria is desert. Mali is the same. But if you walk in one desert you don't notice the same things as in the other desert. The desert in Mali is strewn with bodies. There, it's much easier to die than to live. There, the wind attaches itself to you and your foot sinks deep into the sand. In Algeria, the way is marked for lorries, for buses, for pickup trucks, for everything. And it's marked for you too. Some paved roads cross the desert, and along those roads there are small villages, small Algerian villages. With houses made of mud, dirt streets, a mosque, and a fountain. There, you can fill your water gourd and continue on your way.

I continued for six days, on foot. From Ouargla to Ghardaïa. One hundred and ninety *kilo* without anything to eat. To drink, yes: water. But that's not a big problem for me, because I know now that hunger doesn't kill a person, nor does pain. To kill a person, you need something else.

Sometimes I am thinking things out, and I ask myself, *What's worse, hunger or pain?* And I conclude: *Of the two, I'd say that hunger is the worst, yes, definitely, hunger.* That's because hunger has no shame: when you're hungry, you'll do anything to find something to eat. When you're in pain, you can wait a little, you have to be patient.

But not all pains require the same kind of patience.

7

Tooth pain. The toothache first got to me in Zawiya, in the chicken hangar. And then it followed me to Ghardaïa. I'd say to myself, *Is this pain never going to forget about me and leave me alone?* I became desperate, because the pain didn't move. It was the same all day and all night. I couldn't get to sleep anymore.

I went looking for some kind of medication, but I didn't have any money and no one gave me any. "It'll pass," they said to me, but it didn't pass. I began to wish for death, more and more as the days went by. I even prayed that I would die. Yes. I prayed. I didn't want to remain here on earth anymore. Why? *There you are, the dead,* I thought. *You're at peace. No one is going to molest you, no one is going to beat you, no one is going to insult you. On top of that, you won't go hungry, and you won't need to drink any water.* I thought all that out.

I walked along the streets, and I began to look for some string. "I need some sort of string," I told people, "very thin but as strong as a rope." They didn't understand me. And the people who passed by me behaved as if I wasn't there, or as if I was mute. "*Jaarama buy.*" I spent the whole day in Ghardaïa looking for string, but it was in vain. No one heard me and no one helped me.

In the end, I went back to Ivu's shelter. Ivu is from the Ivory Coast, and he works in a *trankilo* in Ghardaïa. As

I went in, I saw a long rug, a little bit like that carpet you see over there, but longer. There were some loose threads sticking out at the ends. They weren't well sewn on, and they were beginning to get loose. With a little strength, I was able to pull one of them along the whole length of the rug and, in that way, end up with a long thread. *I'll try with that*, I thought, and I began.

One, I made a knot at one end, a *tête de noeud*, a head knot. Two, I opened my mouth and placed the knot firmly around my tooth. *Yes, now that tooth is a prisoner.* Three, I tied the other end of the thread to my foot, like this. And with my leg, I started to pull at the tooth. First to the right and then to the left. Again and again, this way and that. I repeated these movements many times. The tooth moved one way and the other, like a child's swing, but it didn't want to come out. *I know*, I thought, and I put my foot on the ground and stood up straight. *Krak.* It fell to the ground. The tooth. The whole tooth with the string still attached to it.

The day after, my face started to blow up, exactly like one of those inflatable Zodiacs. It swelled along my cheek and up to my forehead. One eye completely disappeared, sunk under the swelling, imprisoned there, and I couldn't open it. I walked around like that for two or three weeks. Eventually, the air under the skin went down, and the pain in my mouth began very slowly to disappear.

Now that I was healed, I thought, *I must start to work.* I went to the place where you can find work, the place little

Ismail had shown me before. An old man came towards me and asked me if I knew how to mix cement. I answered yes, of course, "*Bien sûr.*"

I spent the whole week in Ghardaïa, sweating, mixing cement. But that sweat gave me strength. By strength, what I want to say is that it gave me the desire to continue living. I started earning a little money, and I also started to understand that I might even be able to find a place for myself in that world.

But the world always has other places, and there was a man next to me with whom I mixed cement.

"There's more work in Algiers than there is here," he said to me, "and they pay better."

"*Oke*," I thanked him, and when I finished work, I went to the station.

From Ghardaïa to Algiers: a thousand and two hundred dinars. I left Ghardaïa at twenty-one hours zero zero, and at the break of day, I found myself in Algiers.

8

I want to go back a little, because I forgot to tell you something about Ghardaïa. I want to tell you about it now. It's not easy to explain, but it's very important for me to try. If I could speak like Emi, I could express it easily, but I am

Ibrahima and I want to speak with my own words. Let's see if you can understand me.

Before I went to Libya, I knew a lot of people in Ghardaïa. However, when I came back from Libya, a lot of them didn't know me anymore. "Ibrahima's gone crazy," they started to say. I never said anything, but I heard everything. "Ibrahima is crazy now," that's what people were saying.

Before I went to Libya, I spoke easily and I had a good sense of humour. But the person who came back from Libya was a mute. My teeth hurt. And so did my head. And the pain in my head was spread through my whole body. To be precise, I had two pains in my head. One was Alhassane and the second, my mother. *How am I going to find the words to explain the* naufrage *to our mother? How am I going to convey news of Alhassane to her?* As I started imagining her answer, I was thinking, *Really, right now, being alive doesn't hold any interest for me anymore.*

And I never said anything. And I never did anything. I remained lying down, or maybe sitting. And I heard, "Yes, Ibrahima is crazy now."

One day, a friend of mine found me and he said to me, "Ibrahima, today I've learned something."

"What?" I asked him.

"I've realised people are talking about you in the *trankilo* and they are saying that you've gone crazy."

"Yes," I reassured him. "That's right, you heard right, and so?"

He told me it wasn't so.

"Yes, it is so," I explained to him. "It's just as they say. I'm becoming a crazy person. And so? Is that a problem for you?"

"No, no problem." He was quiet.

And then I went on to ask him, "Have you got a cigarette?"

"Yes."

"Well, give it to me, please."

I lit the cigarette and I remained silent. That's what it is to be crazy: you don't have the strength for anything, other people don't interest you. You only want to be left alone.

Here, as well, I'm often alone, and I ask myself, *How can I continue living with the life I have?* I'm focusing on this question, but then I begin to look at those around me, to my left and to my right. My father often said this: "Whatever happens, you will always be in the middle. There will be someone ahead of you and there will be someone behind you. That's what life is like, and you can never ever say: I'm suffering more than anyone else."

9

Do you see that boy sitting over there, on the wooden bench?

That is Ousmane. He arrived here two months ago. In the refuge, he's always getting into fights; he can't find any peace. He doesn't say a word all day long, except to ask for a cigarette. Just that. He's forgotten everything else. Everyone says he's crazy. Yes, crazy. That's an easy word. But I understand him.

Because I know what it's like when your spirit is spinning out of control, and when that starts it's not easy to get yourself back. There are a lot of people like that, I've seen them. In Libya, in Algeria, in Morocco. People who are lost, without hope; they'd rather be dead, but they're alive. They live without knowing who they're living for, or what they're living for. And here too, it's the same.

Look. There's Ousmane, he's here today as well. Do you see him, on his wooden bench? What could he be thinking about? Will he ever be able to forget everything he remembers?

We saw so many bodies along the way. Some in the desert, others in the sea. The dead remain there; we keep on moving. That's the only difference. But our movements are ordered by someone else. "Go there," they say to us, and we go there. "Come here," they say to us, and we come here. No questions asked. Days pass. Sitting on a bench. Smoking a cigarette. Until someone offers us something else.

Your balance hangs by such a thin thread, and it's very difficult to keep that thread from breaking. And that's why today I'm sitting next to Ousmane, and I say to him: "Don't let go, Ousmane, hang on in there." I try to be sensitive to the changes he is going through. But he answers: "*Koto*, my life cannot ever again be repaired." And I remain silent, because I understand Ousmane. What he's saying and what he's not saying. That kind of suffering cannot be fixed by anyone.

If you were suffering like that, you too would become ill. Your head would leave your body on one of those wooden benches and wander elsewhere. Maybe for good. People would pass you by, and they'd say that you're crazy. Yes, they use that word, "crazy." But there needs to be another word. Crazy is too easy a word to use.

I O

"What you need, Ibrahima, is to find a little love," a friend said to me one day. "You need to find somebody, somebody whose hand you can hold and who will connect you back to life."

"I know," I answered. "That's something I would like as well, and even one day I'd like to start a family, that's my greatest hope. But at the moment, I can't. There are too many worries inside my body."

And that's the way it is. People here can't believe it, but ever since I left my village, I haven't had any physical relationship with anyone. I haven't been looking for anyone. And no one has tried to find me either. That's how it is, *tout simplement.* When I was living in the woods, sometimes a woman came to me and asked, "Ibrahima, could you go and fetch some water for us?" I always answered "Of course." And I'd go. I always tried to help the women in any way I could, but if there was something I couldn't do, I would say, "No, no, that's not possible."

If you have some kind of intention in your head, your heart can develop it and then it will start searching for something. But if you don't even think about anything, your heart remains silent, stuck, and the wish isn't there. And actually, to tell you the truth, I don't have much experience in that area, but it doesn't bother me, it really doesn't. The only thing that bothers me is my own life. When and where I can see my mother again. And what she will think when she sees me.

Inside my head, that is all there is.

I I

Forgive me, I've lost the thread. Where were we?

. . . Ah, yes, Algiers.

I spent a year and three months in Algiers, in the Birkhadem suburb. That's more or less five hundred days. And I spent every day with my three friends: water, sand, and cement. I had three items of clothing as well. One shovel and two gloves. I bought the gloves myself, because my hands were getting damaged. And in Birkhadem, if your hands got ruined, there were always other hands arriving to do the work. They arrived from Mali, Nigeria, Cameroon, from all over. Every day, more and more arrived. All migrants. They had crossed the desert from Southern Africa, or they were escaping the war in Syria. It's really very simple and logical: if there's hard work to be done, the migrants will do it.

The work in Birkhadem had to be half-hidden so that the police wouldn't suspect anything. We couldn't even leave the worksite at night, it was too dangerous. There was a large block where they kept the cement mixer, and we slept under there, hidden. That was our bed: a little bit of concrete. And that was our mattress: a little bit of cardboard. And then, at first light: rise, pray, fold up the cardboard, and start work.

I know nothing about Algiers outside of that worksite. In the Arab quarters, they despised us. If I entered a shop because I had to buy something, they chased me out with a "No animals are allowed in here." I heard insults when I was simply walking on the pavement. And some people didn't even say anything, they just held their noses as I walked past them.

Going into the Arab quarters means being subjected to continual humiliation. Not only from the police, but from ordinary people as well—people like you and me, often even children. And you can't demand anything else. There is nothing you can say.

12

Algiers has three stations. One is for trains, the other for taxis, and the last one for buses. The name of the bus station is Kharouba. That's where I bought a ticket for Oran.

From Algiers to Oran, eight hundred dinars, six hours.

As I was getting off the bus, a man approached me and before even saying, "Good morning," he said to me: "If you want, I can help you get to Morocco. I'm very familiar with the ways to get there."

He was a people-smuggler, but he wasn't an Arab.

"*Je suis du Gabon*, I'm from Gabon," he said to me, "and I've been in Algeria for some years."

At first, I trusted him, but after giving me a little information, he asked for one hundred euros. "That's the price of my work."

"Excuse me," I answered him, "but I won't pay anything until I actually get to Morocco."

"That's the way everyone else does it," he said angrily. "You have to do the same as others do."

"No," I insisted. "If you believed in your work, it would be all the same to you if you got paid now or when we got there." And I showed him my money, one hundred euros, in Algerian dinars.

He thought for a little while. "*Oke,*" he answered. "We'll leave this afternoon."

We took a train, even now I don't know where to. We got off the train in a small village. There were forty-four of us. All of them people like me. "From here, we have to go on foot," said the man from Gabon. "And in the middle of the mountains, our traces will be lost." And then I understood: *We won't have to jump over any barriers. We'll go from Algeria to Morocco through the mountains.*

Mohamed Salah is a long and deep canyon. We call it "a tunnel," but in France, they call it "*le canyon.*" People who have vertigo can't go there, because you have to walk along a precipice. It's extremely dangerous. Ordinary people aren't used to walking in that kind of place. Nor are the police.

We walked for two whole nights, following on the heels of our people-smuggler. During the day, we hid in the woods. When the sun went down, we started walking again. "Moroccan searchlights travel far, and they control everything from the top of the mountains," the man from Gabon warned us. "We have to be very careful."

At a certain point, as the mountains unfolded before us, something appeared along the side of the canyon, a narrow shaft of light. It was the signal to say we were approaching a small paved road. And there, an old minibus was waiting for us. It would take us to Oujda, in Morocco.

As I was getting on the minibus, a hand stopped me. "And my money?" he asked.

13

From Oujda to Tangiers is a long way, much too far to do it on foot. My feet, as they are now, aren't made for walking so much. When they're starting to go somewhere, they remember the desert and they start to swell up again. Especially the right foot. And then I have to stop.

"The bus station is behind that square," an old man explained to me. "*Oke*," I answered. And I took the bus to Tangiers. I can't remember how much it cost, but I can remember how long it took. We left Oujda at nine twenty, and we arrived in Tangiers at nineteen zero zero.

I spent the first night in the station, lying on a bench. I didn't know Tangiers at all.

The next morning, someone come up to me and explained: "Here, people like you and me live in the woods."

"Really?"

"Yes."

"*Oke.*"

And I went into the woods. It was the time of *Suumayee*. In our language, *Suumayee* is the word for Ramadan.

In the woods of Tangiers, all the separate communities have their own space. There, you have the Ivory Coast; over there, Nigeria; Cameroon, there; and us, here. By us here, I mean that this was Guinea. We were mostly Muslims, but no one was able to respect the fast—it was impossible. In the forest, you have to eat when you can, at night or during the day. Our religion knows this and accepts it.

In the Guinean community, we gathered together five dirhams, and at nightfall someone would go to the town to look for food. Coming out of the woods into the town was dangerous, but it's not easy to live without food. Your stomach hurts. But hunger doesn't know fear; when you're hungry you'll do anything to eat. Sometimes I was the one who had to go to the town. When we returned, there was a fire ready, and the women cooked the food. And then we all ate together—men, women, and the children.

14

I've been talking about stomachaches. That's quite an adventure as well, and I know all about it.

The pain didn't start in Tangiers; it was already with me when I was in Algiers. Since the day I was born I had never felt such torment, and I thought to myself: *A man is going to disappear soon.* By *a man*, I meant that man, me, but the pain was also me: it was all of me, completely. It wasn't only my stomach: it started from my back and went all the way down to my legs. It's as if you were to get hold of a pair of pliers and twist the intestines.

It was impossible for me to go to the hospital there. Morocco is not like here. Here, they take you to the Accident and Emergency unit, and the doctor says, "We'll have to open this up today." That's what they did to me here: they put me to sleep, and I woke up with twenty stitches in my stomach. I had a stomach ulcer. But in Algeria and Morocco, you can't go to an Accident and Emergency unit. They throw you out of the hospital and they say to you, "Go back to your own country, this is no place for you." That's why I was living with such agonising stomach pains and kept thinking to myself: *A man is going to disappear soon.*

One day, in the woods, a friend came to me and said: "Ibrahima, I've called on a certain *marabout*."

In Africa, a *marabout* is a person who knows the secrets of the Koran. He knows about the Koran and he knows about the body, but he's not a doctor—he's never been inside a school.

I said no to my friend. "It'll pass."

"No, Ibrahima." He was obstinate. "I can see the agony in your eyes, and I'm going right now to find the *marabout*."

Five minutes later, the two of us were there together in the woods. I was from Guinea and he was from Niger. I was the stomachache; he was the *marabout*. He asked me two or three questions, and he started doing his *marabout*ing.

One, he touched my stomach. Two, he moved my arms. And three, he closed his eyes. When your eyes are closed, you can think better.

"Ibrahima, how is your pain?" he asked me.

"I haven't felt such agony since my own mother brought me into this world," I answered.

"*Oke*," he said, "if you want your pain to go away, you have to eat a certain herb, and the name of that herb is . . ."

Sorry, but I've forgotten the name of the herb. And yet, I knew it . . . It doesn't matter. In the end, I didn't believe in it, and I told him my body wasn't used to eating such things.

"Ibrahima, this is your medication," he repeated. "If you want to get better, that's what you have to eat."

"*Oke*," I answered, "thank you."

But I didn't eat it. When you have a terrible pain in your body, it occupies your whole body and you forget all the other pains. I knew exactly what pain would reappear once my stomachache passed. "Alhassane, *miñan* . . ." But the cure for that kind of pain isn't a herb that you can find in a wood. I knew this, and I didn't need a *marabout* to tell me what I already knew.

And so, the stomachache accompanied me from Algiers to Morocco. In Oujda, it kept me company for three days, and then for many more days in Tangiers. It would be the same in Nador. But there was nothing I could do, because the hospitals there are not like the ones here. If you're a migrant there, they show you the door and they say, "Go back home, you don't belong here."

And in the meantime, the pliers continue to twist your intestines.

15

I remained in Tangiers for three months, on guard twenty-four hours a day, always trembling with fear. The police came into the woods almost every day, and then we had to escape into the mountains, all of us. Cameroonians, Malians, Ivoirians, and us, the Guineans: the whole of Africa was running away. Pursuing us were the Moroccan police, with their sticks, their blows, their insults. As for us, we kept running.

"Stop, *taburdimok,* stop!"

In the end, they caught me. Twice. I still have the wounds to show for it. Can you see? Wait, I'll lift my trouser leg a bit. There. That one happened when I started running away but fell into a hole. My leg got stuck in the fissure of a rock. The police ended up having to break up the rock with a hammer so that I could get my leg out. Once they'd done that, they emptied my pockets, and then they put me on a bus and sent me to Tiznit. "Don't ever come back here," they said. "*Oke*," I answered.

But I went back. Tiznit–Casablanca–Tangiers, eight hundred dirhams, fourteen hours. I took the bus and paid with my own money. The Moroccan police may have beat me with their sticks and emptied my pockets, but they were never able to find any money on me. They found a bag with the photograph of my little brother and a Sony Ericsson phone. But they didn't find money. I had made this decision: *If I die, the money will decompose with my body and no one will ever find it.*

I'm the only who knows where I was hiding it.

If you want, I'll tell you. Otherwise, you'll start imagining all sorts of things and think something completely different. That often happens, you know. I'll tell you now so that you won't get it wrong.

Do you see these trousers? Yes, these jeans. At the ankle, there's a narrow fold, and there the jeans are sewn twice, there are two layers of cloth here. Look carefully and you'll see that your jeans are the same. I think all jeans are made the same way. Can you see? If you open this hem here, and break the thread, you can put something inside. Maybe some bills, rolled up like a cigarette. *Voilà.* Then you have to close up the hem without anyone seeing you do it. You sew it with a thread, little by little. And the bills are there, imprisoned, until the moment you need them.

That's what I did. And that's how I was able to pay the fare and return to Tangiers by bus.

16

"The European *program* in Nador is cheaper than the one here." That's what a Malian told me one day in Tangiers. I immediately had my doubts and wondered: *If it's really cheaper there, then why are you still here?* I didn't believe him. Even so, I went to Nador.

Nador is farther from Europe than Tangiers, but the woods there are much more extensive. I don't know mathematically how many different woods there are in Nador: maybe eight, maybe twelve. The woods are all the same, but some have their own name, for example, Afra, or Buzunbura. The name of our wood was Peau Blanc.

I spent six months there, one hundred and eighty days, without doing anything. There, in the woods, you're simply one more tree. And it's winter. Rain, wind, cold. A piece of cardboard. Or maybe two pieces. You lie down, you remain there, you don't move, like the cold itself.

Sometimes the police come. You leave your piece of cardboard and you're off, running. *Stop, taburdimok, stop.*

But Nador is not like Tangiers. The Nador police get tired more quickly; they give up and leave the wood—until the next day. "*Au revoir.*" And then you go back to your piece of cardboard and you sit. Or you lie down. You remain there. You don't move. And it's winter.

The people-smugglers asked us to pay them four thousand euros, or sometimes three thousand five hundred. At the very least, very very least, three thousand. The *tonbola* isn't cheap, and it's dangerous.

There were some who, out of desperation, tried to work miracles: with the *ramer-ramer*, or rowing-rowing. Four or five people would pool their money and buy a small plastic inflatable boat. They would get hold of some wooden paddles and set off. They asked me to join them a couple of times, but I said no. I thought: *That program may only cost a hundred euros, but it's incredibly risky. If water gets into the inflatable boat, that's it, that's the end.*

I learned recently that some friends I left in the woods had done this and lost their lives in the sea. I received the news through Messenger.

17

When you live in the woods, whether in Tangiers or Nador, there's always another wood, which you can't see, because everyone stays in their own place, alone, inside their own body. People are silent, no one ever says anything, but you can look into their eyes and assume that there is something else, inside them, something that can't escape. You can dodge the police fairly easily, but this other thing, never.

By this other thing what I want to say is everyone's particular story.

I never had any intention of embarking on an adventure. I was learning to drive a truck and I thought that, after a while, I could do that as a profession. With a job like that, I could support my family without ever having to leave Guinea. That was my goal. But my little brother went missing, and my whole destiny suddenly changed.

I called my mother from Algeria. It was a Friday. I explained to her that she wouldn't be able to see Alhassane again, and she started screaming and crying. At that time, Mother cried a lot. Afterwards, I don't know. The telephone credit ran out, and we couldn't finish our talk. And when the line was cut, I too began to cry because of how much I loved that child.

That's why, when I say "this other thing," what I want to say is someone's story. Someone's dreams and mistakes, all mixed up. And that, that other thing, remains silent, very silent, inside each person, inside another wood.

Here too that *other thing* attacks me every day, and I'm afraid. I'm afraid I'll also lose my little sisters, Rouguiatou and Binta. Before I left home, it was easy for me to explain things to them, to tell them not to move far from the house. They listened to everything I said and they always agreed with me. But it's been a long time since I've left home, and everything has changed.

That's why, whenever I can, I call my mother and I ask, "Mother, are my little sisters all right?" And then my mother hands over the phone to my little sisters and they ask me, "Ibrahima, do you still remember us?"

18

If I ever go back home and if my mother and my little sisters are still there, I would like to tell them everything, in the same way I've been telling you. So that they too can understand me a little. At the moment, they know nothing. And if I started to tell them now, the telephone credit would soon run out because my story is such a long one and the credit is so short. But one day, yes, if I ever return, and they're still there, we'll sit next to each other and I'll tell them everything.

First, Mali. Then, Libya. *Taf-taf* and the torture. Yes, that's what happened to me as I was looking for Alhassane. But he, my little brother, embarked on a Zodiac and went on the sea. One hundred and forty-three people, and him. I didn't know anything. But one

Friday, as I returned from prayer, the meaning of the word *"naufrage"* was explained to me. And I understood. *"C'est fini."* That's the end. Alhassane has slipped through my hands and is gone.

Like a piece of Kleenex. Just like that.

That's how I'll describe everything that happened, and I know what they'll ask me. Why didn't I return home if my destiny wasn't to go to Europe? I often ask myself the same thing, and I don't find it easy to explain. But I'll tell you. One: when you're feeling the heavy weight of guilt on your shoulders, it's hard to see your way clearly. Two: once I'd arrived in Morocco or Libya, it felt too late to turn back, home is too far away, and that stops you. You're caught between the desert and the sea, like a trapped animal. And three: I don't deserve to find myself in front of my mother; I'm not worthy to be seen by her. That thought keeps running through my head.

And that's why it's been some time since I've prayed. The last time I prayed was when I was being brought to the *tonbola.* Yes. There. I was getting into the boat, without the *guba.* I prayed and I thought, *If God wants me to go to Europe, I will go to Europe. And if he doesn't want that, then I'll get lost at sea.*

Yes, me too.

19

"I don't have that much money."

That's what I said to the people-smugglers who came into the woods. They thought that I was lying, that I was simply refusing to pay the full price. But it was the truth, I did not have three thousand euros. I had arrived in Nador with two thousand and six hundred euros. And so we never agreed on a price, and they went away, the people-smugglers with their *programs*. Every time. They left, and they didn't come back.

Not all the smugglers were Arabs. They were some of our ethnicity, on their way to Europe; they had a good sense of business and had established themselves in Morocco. In order to undertake that kind of business, you have to have a very small heart. That's not a problem, it's even necessary, but not everyone can do that. Maybe you can learn to be that way, little by little, I don't know. I never tried.

One day, someone by the name of Bahry came into the wood. He was a Guinean and he spoke Pulaar. He too wanted three thousand euros, like all the others, but I explained my situation to him and he took the time to listen. He told me that at that time he couldn't help me, but when a little time had passed, ten days or maybe fifteen, he'd give me an answer. "*Oke,*" I said to him, "I'm not moving from here."

More than two months went by, and I didn't see Bahry again. I had written his telephone number on a piece of paper, and I called from a phone that belonged to one of my friends, but there was no answer. In the end, I gave up and I thought, *This wood is my home now. I'll never get out of here.*

I think it was a Wednesday or maybe a Thursday, I'm not sure, but I saw Bahry again. He came into the wood with two Moroccans. They were preparing a *program*, and they were looking for clients. They were asking for three thousand five hundred euros, and people were trying to make them lower the price, to maybe three thousand and two hundred, or even just three thousand. But when the wood is full of desperate people, it's not easy to do that. If you say no to the price, there are plenty of people behind you who'll agree to it. That's how business works.

When he'd finished his round, Bahry came up to me.

"How are you?" he asked.

And I said, "*Jam tun.*"

"Ibrahima," he said. "I don't have a *program* for you, but I have something else."

"What?"

"If you want, you can come to my house and stay there until the next *program* is ready."

I left the wood, I got into his car, and he took me to his apartment. Bahry lived in a neighbourhood of Nador. He had a kitchen, a room, and a sitting room. I slept in the sitting room, on a sofa, and my back was really surprised by that: for over two years I had only ever lain down on cement or on the hard ground in the woods.

When I woke up, I prepared breakfast for everyone. Everyone meant Bahry and his wife. "When breakfast is finished," he said to me, "you'll start cleaning. The work that is usually done by housewives is what I expect you to do here."

"*Oke*," I answered.

I stayed for three months in that little apartment, without ever going outside.

20

And then one morning: "Ibrahima, I'm preparing a *program* today," Bahry told me. "I'm going to pray to God that it will be safe, and I'd like you to take that boat as well."

"*Oke*, it's not a problem," I answered.

We agreed on two thousand euros. That was what my trip cost. Two thousand euros, and three months in their house doing all the housework.

That night, he brought me to the seashore. They were putting air into the Zodiac. There were nine holes, and everyone had to work without stopping, using hand pumps, crouching down and pumping, pumping, pumping, pumping. I can still hear the music of the pumping in my ears: *ful-ful-ful-ful-ful.* Everything always has to be done at the last moment. The Zodiac is inflated, the motor attached to the boat, a compass is brought, the boat is pushed into the water. And off you go. No, wait. Not yet. I forgot something.

The Moroccan police have some large projectors, and they can control everything from the top of a mountain. They saw us as well, as we were about to leave, and they started to shout. And so the Arabs, without even pausing for breath, continued pumping, *ful-ful-ful-ful-ful.* Those Arabs are very skilful at doing that.

For security, the Zodiac has to be very well inflated. Sometimes, at sea, it can suddenly lose air. And more often than not, a Zodiac takes more people than it should. *Ful-ful-ful-ful-ful.* We were fifty-three people on the boat. Children, women and men.

So: the motor is attached, a compass is brought on board, the Zodiac is pushed into the water—and off you go. Yes, now. And from now on, you're in the grip of chance.

You look in all four directions, and everywhere it's exactly the same: the sea. And you've never sat on a boat before. And then the motor stops. Maybe the captain has decided to change the speed, or maybe something else— who knows what?—but the motor has stopped.

They started to pull on the cord, they pulled, they pulled, and they pulled. They pulled with desperation. Finally, the motor started up again, and we kept going, further and further away from the shore. And there, again, you look in all directions and again, it's the same: the sea. And you don't know how to swim. And at that moment, the compass gives up.

Before we left, the Arabs had explained this much to us: "If the boat remains between zero and fifteen degrees, you're going the right way. But if the needle passes between fifteen and thirty degrees, it's not the right way." And I don't know what happened, but suddenly someone said, "The compass isn't working." And so now, we were going ahead without being able to check the numbers on the compass. We had no idea what direction we were going in.

We were lost in the middle of the sea.

And there, again, you look in all four directions, and again, it's the same: the sea. But then, some pieces of flesh suddenly start jumping out of the water, *Ohhhhhhh*. They rise and then they go back down, *Ohhhhhh*. Someone said, "*Des dauphins*, dolphins." But I had never heard that word before, and I was terrified. I thought they would come and leap onto the boat.

Ohhhhhhhh . . .

My spirit started to fly away into the air. *It was on a night like this that Alhassane left*, I thought. And I started remembering my whole family. First, Father; then, Mother; and last, my two little sisters still at home, Binta and Rouguiatou.

When you're sitting like that on the sea, you find yourself in the middle of a crossing: one way is life, one way is death. At sea, there's no other way out.

21

We spent the whole night drifting at sea, in the middle of nowhere. People started crying. Mostly the women, but not only the women—the captain started crying as well. He was Senegalese. I don't know who put him in charge of our expedition. He said he had experience of the sea, but a captain needs to have a stronger heart, he needs to show courage. This one was crying like a little child. It's hard to reach Europe if you behave like that.

I tried to keep the wings of my spirit attached to me, not to think anymore, but it wasn't easy. I kept seeing the face of my mother in front of my eyes. And I kept thinking: *It was on a night like this that Alhassane left.*

The sea is vast, like the night. But with the night, you know that if you wait a little, you will come to the end of it and then it will be day, and the light will appear. But then, the vast and endless expanse of the sea reveals itself once more, and you think, *Impossible. It's impossible.*

And just at that moment, the Zodiac started to lose air. The captain ordered everyone to move to one side, and the boat almost capsized. Everyone was screaming and then crying. And so was I. I felt terror penetrate deep into my bones. And again, for the last time, I looked in all four directions, and everywhere I saw the same thing: the sea. Impossible.

Some put on the vests, the *gubas* that they had brought with them. Others had the inner tubes of bicycle tyres around their bodies, which they had inflated. I hadn't brought anything, and that was an extra worry weighing on me. But then I also realised I had carried with me much less hope than the others had.

Eleven zero zero. Everything the same.

Twelve zero zero, and I remained there, waiting for death. And then I pinched the Zodiac with my fingers, and I realised there wasn't that much air in it. The Zodiac was deflating, and would soon have no air left in it at all.

Thirteen zero zero. Everything the same. I continued to wait for death.

22

Fourteen zero zero: a helicopter. First you hear it, then you see it, and in the end, you believe it. Yes, it's a helicopter.

The two girls next to me took off their *gubas* and gave them to me. I started waving them in the air. To the left and to the right. And again, to the left and to the right. Others started doing the same. Those were our signals: all the *gubas* were dancing above our heads. "Help us! Help us!"

The helicopter descended towards us and started circling over us. The propellers caused waves in the sea, and the Zodiac almost capsized. And we were all screaming: "Help us! Help us!"

They saw us. They made a gesture with their hands, and then they went away. And at that moment, I gave up. The memory of my mother came back to me. *She's there, in her village, what is she doing now?* When the helicopter disappeared, the hope that I could come out of this alive and in one piece abandoned me.

Forty minutes later, the helicopter came back. First the helicopter, and then a boat. *Salvamento maritimo*, sea rescue. I recognised the colour. In the woods, they had explained to me what that colour meant: "If a boat comes to rescue you, it will have the same colour as an orange." And so it was. We all started to shout: "*Boza! Boza! Boza!*"

That shout is part of a song that Africans sing among themselves. It's always sung when an adventure at sea comes to a happy end. "*Boza! Boza! Boza!* Whether in the woods of Tangiers or of Nador, when people heard that a *program* had made it safely to the shores of Europe, the news spread far and wide: "Yesterday, a hundred people sang *Boza!*"

23

The *Salvamento* boat stopped next to ours, and they offered us a long rope. First the children and the women were lifted off the Zodiac. We were all shouting, asking for our turn. "*Tranquilo, tranquilo,*" they kept saying to us from the ship. I know a lot of words of French, and I immediately thought, *Those words mean we have to remain calm.* And so I made myself quiet down a little.

My turn came. With a long rope, they lifted me from the Zodiac onto the rescue boat, and they brought me a blanket and some water. I drank a mouthful, and I started to cry. I was crying like a little child. Then I got up, and I looked around me. I wanted to see where I had come from.

I know now that if you want somewhere to sit, the sea is not the right place.

And you, the one I've addressed so many
times
you will be wondering who you are.

You are, possibly, the police
a commissioner in front of a big desk
you're determining my right to asylum
you will decide
what to do with me.

Or you are, perhaps, my mother
Fatimatu Diallo
I've cheated you of so many words
forgive me if
I have not told you all of this until now.

Or you are Fatumata Binta
or you are Rouguiatou
and I want you to know
that Ibrahima has not forgotten you.

But in this story you are so many more,

you are Ismail
you are Emi
I am asking if you are still alive today
and what has been your fate.

Or you are, maybe
someone who is at this moment crossing the
desert
or waiting in the woods for word of a
program,
for you as well there is much information here.

Or you are someone who has helped me to
get here
In Oran or in Irun
you are so many.

Or very simply
you are you
and you are reading this poem at this
moment.

And you will say,
you there, am I you?

Yes
if you want
you are the one there.

But not I
I am Ibrahima
and this is my life.

About the Authors

Ibrahima Balde is a migrant from the Republic of Guinea who crossed the desert to look for his younger brother. After entering the European Union without papers, he made his way to the Basque Country, where, while living in a homeless shelter in Irun, he met Amets Arzallus. Ibrahima has applied for asylum and now lives in a Red Cross hostel in Madrid.

Amets Arzallus, a child of refugees, is a well-known Basque improvisational poet who works with an association that supports migrants in the Basque Country.

Timberlake Wertenbaker is an award-winning British playwright.